Echoes in the Stream of Time

A
Gothic
Adventure
Gamebook

By Dario Nardi

FROM THE AUTHOR

This gamebook, the second in a series, takes you deeper toward a great unseen horror. This 1930's-ish parallel of our own world blends electrotech, magic, monsters, and psychology. This time around, you will play along in a new place and follow a new hero with a different personality. As a young airman, you will have a mix of allies, competition, and several romantic options. The ride starts with a gentle mystery, takes unsettling turns, and culminates in horrors akin to book one. I hope you enjoy.

Written by Dario Nardi, Copyright July 2, 2019.

Cover art by Eric Lofgren. The scene depicted appears on page 138. Design by Dario Nardi. Proofreading by Keith Mageau.

Published by: Radiance House
PO Box 691971, Los Angeles, CA, 90069
www.RadianceHouse.com
service@RadianceHouse.com

ISBN: 978-1-5136-5364-8

CONTENTS

How to Play

Echoes in the Stream of Time is an adventure gamebook. That is, the book is organized into dozens of scenes, and you progress through scenes as a character—a Royal Air Force Special Lieutenant—to complete a quest. The quest is to solve the mystery of what happened to the vanished crew of a spellship (magical airplane). Ideally, you also earn a promotion. You start at scene #1, make choices and take chances as you face challenges, and hopefully survive to victory at the end.

To play, you will need a pencil or pen, a copy of your "character sheet" (page 6), at least one standard (6-sided) die, plus a 20-sided ("d20") die, and optionally, graph paper. If you lack a d20, you can roll three standard dice and total the results.

Who Are You?

You have two choices to make before starting. First, choose your character's proud **name**. Second, choose your **gifts**. That is, there are six attributes and your character excels at two. There is Brawn, Endurance, Agility, Intellect, Faith, and Charm. Every scene requires you use one, and all six are equally useful in play. You will surely shine in scenes requiring your gifts.

Your character has two measures of health: **vitality** points and **sanity** points. Vitality tracks your body and wounds that you suffer. Sanity tracks your mind and the impact of your job's horrors. In many scenes, you may lose points. If you drop below 0 vitality, you die. If you drop below 0 sanity, you go insane. Either way, the adventure is over. Fortunately, you have potions for your body and bitter tea for your spirit. You can drink these after any scene to regain some points unless stated otherwise. You will also have chances to rest, a magical comic book tattoo if you fall below 0 vitality, and other recovery options such as healing wands. Just be mindful. Facing the supernatural is a dangerous job!

Finally, your character can cast a dozen minor spells that conjure light, improve aim, locate objects, and so on. These ease your job. You will learn how spells work early in the adventure.

Resolving Scenes

Each scene starts with descriptive text. After that text, you might have a choice to skip the scene but usually, you continue into it and select a tactical option. Read carefully! Then you learn which attribute the scene demands such as Brawn or Charm, and you roll a d20, add modifiers as stated, and look up the result. Based on the result, you pass or fail. If you fail, you suffer a consequence and usually then go on to success, but sometimes you may be tasked to keep rolling dice until you pass. Finally, you might get to choose where to go next. Often, you will go to the very next scene, but you may be able to jump ahead several scenes or choose between two or three versions of a scene (such as for romantic partners). Your choices involve trade-offs in vitality, sanity, and so forth.

As you go, you may find treasure: special, useful items. You can use these to unlock certain scenes or improve your chances of survival. You may also earn **boons**, which are divine blessings that you can use to improve your chances.

Multiple Players

This book assumes solo play. Optionally, two to four people can play. One person can read the text as a guide while another rolls dice and makes choices. Or, two or three people can play Junior Lieutenants, each with different gifts. With multiple heroes, each has half or a third the usual vitality and sanity, as stated on the character sheet, and players pick who tackles which scenes based on their gifts, sanity, and vitality. The "off" player can lend aid by rolling 1d6 and adding the result to the

CHARACTER SHEET

Player: _____   **Date**: _____

Character Name: Special Lieutenant (Charlie or Charlene) Ernest
(Note: For 2 or 3 players, each is "Jr. Special Lieutenant" with a name.)

Your Gifts (circle two):
    Brawn   Agility   Faith
    Endurance   Intellect   Charm
(Note: You enjoy a +3 bonus on d20 rolls involving your gifts.)

Vitality Points: Max 30 ; Now [ ]
(Note: For 2 or 3 players, each has Max 15 or 10 vitality points.)

Sanity Points: Max 10 ; Now [ ]
(Note: For 2 or 3 players, each has Max 5 or 3 sanity points.)

Treasure value: 30 coins worth

Investigator Gear: Royal Air Force uniform, ID card, shotgun, box of shells, holy symbol, forensic toolkit, analyzer wand, lie detector, UV black light, batteries, flashlight, lighter, hunting knife, comic book, mirror, box of condoms, amulet to detect magic, and basic spell dust.

Expendable Gear:
Healing potion (+1d6 vitality, 3 uses)
Flask of bitter tea (+3 sanity, 8 uses)
Lucky charm (+5 on d20 roll, 1 use)

Special Finds:
_____
_____
_____

Tattoo: You have 1 comic hero tattoo. One time when you fall below 0 vitality, the tattoo heals you to 1 vitality and 1 sanity and then vanishes.

Goals: Determine why the spellship returned with no crew, locate the missing airmen, finger a spy or saboteur, find your mentor Mage Greene, improve your magic, get lucky in romance, earn a promotion.

Boons: Start 0 ; Now [ ]   **Current Scene**: [ ]

others' d20 roll. Also, if one hero's vitality or sanity falls below 0, then a remaining player can revive the fallen ally by using up tea or a healing potion.

THE CURTAIN RISES

The Royal Spellship Redkite left the base as usual this morning. But it never arrived at its destination. Rather, it returned on auto-pilot with no crew. Poof, they vanished, and with them your mentor, the base's old mage. The spellship's secret cargo remains secure, with perplexing clues. Is the answer a saboteur, monster, malfunctioning electrotech, an errant spell, or something weirder?

You are a newly-minted Air Force investigator. Unlike most folks, you know a little magic, and like any smart youth, you are adept with electrotech devices, the wonders of the age. Your trusty wand can scan for life signs and analyze objects, at least while its batteries work. A lie detector is a remarkable contraption, though it requires keen attention and can't catch psychopaths. Of course, you are generally familiar with ergo robots and spellships, those avant-garde hybrids of technology and magic. But even with these, can you survive this mystery?

As a little kid during the Great War, you saw your family snatched by devils—not just by enemy soldiers, but by actual real-life winged, tarry, fiery monsters. On that terrible night, a friendly Air Force squad rescued you, and only you, from a doorway to Hell itself. Orphaned, you grew up at an Air Force base. There, Mage Radulfr Greene took you under his wing and encouraged your seedling gift with magic. That seed isn't much, but it makes you more than a standard issue airman.

You are now a newly-minted Special Lieutenant! Aside from a few simple spells under your belt, your fellow airmen know you to be modest, kind, careful, smart, and a tad spooked. The horrors of that fiendish night long ago would have scarred any child. You possess no photographs of your lost family and barely recall their faces but their love lives on in you. These days, you work at the airbase you grew up at, and it's a solid start. That said, like the comic book heroes you adore reading about, you yearn to fly out of your nest and travel the world. To do that, you must prove your metal and earn a big promotion.

Here's your dirty little secret: You fear that something odd—disorienting, ugly, and perhaps ruinous—nests inside you. You suffer foggy nightmares and see little disturbances at the corners of your vision. Maybe you harbor more than a few minor spells in you? Who or what planted the seed of magic in you anyway? Perhaps a vile force is wiggling up from deep inside, hungry to get out...Or maybe you are simply going a little stir crazy cooped up on base all the time with no love life! After all, you are young, single, a dreamer with too many comic books, and a bit bored with routine... until today.

The larger world is akin to the 1930s with a twist. There are trains, electricity, radio, and similar technologies. Unlike our world, there is a limited measure of magic, just enough that everyone is at least vaguely aware of its benefits and dangers as a means to bend Nature's rules. Miracles of healing and truth may result. There is also mystery and mayhem because monsters are born from magic too. There is a central religion and church that honors the Creator, an all-seeing, all-powerful universal force of law and goodness. Most agree there are lesser gods of all kinds, akin to the Greek and Roman deities, and everyone knows there are angels, demons, and devils, though most folk gladly never meet them. Finally, like our real 1930s, this world wallows in a depression between a Great War a few years back and another likely worse war looming ahead. These wars, aided by magic and monstrous beings, are even worse than the ones we know.

Now, are you ready to prove your courage and skill? Can you figure out what happened to that empty spellship and find its missing crew, including your mentor? Can you earn a pro-motion? Or will you flub your first big assignment, or maybe lose your soul? The first hours of any investigation are crucial. You better get started...

PART I

BAGGAGE & TICKET, PLEASE

Scene #1

Flashback

"You can do it," Mage Greene speaks gently, encouraging you. "Imagine some warmth in your palm."

You are ten years old. Mage Greene is a bald and wiry pea-colored goliath, his head and torso sprinkled with dark runic tattoos. But he's got a jolly smile as he teaches you a spell.

"Ugh," you reply, exasperated. You want to please him. But you also want to give up. The room is shadowy, and darkness feels safer than the light.

"Magic is for monsters," you announce with all the confidence that you can muster. You know this first-hand. When you were six, a band of fiends—with bat-like wings and sulfurous scents, leering eyes and sharp manicured claws—came for your family. Only you were rescued after hiding in the dark.

"Magic's for heroes too," the mage replies. "Captain Avalon, in the comics, can conjure light, can't he?"

"Yeah, like the Captain," you repeat, determined to do well. But you think, you'll never be Captain Avalon.

HOW DO YOU TRY TO CAST THE SPELL?
DO YOU FOCUS ON 1) WARMING YOUR HAND,
2) PLEASING THE MAGE, 3) LIGHTING UP THE ROOM,
OR 4) CAPTAIN AVALON FIGHTING FIENDS?

You rub your palms together again, warming them, and then place your right hand on your heart while holding out your left, palm up and open, focusing on its warmth. The Captain did it differently, but as the mage had once explained, "You'll surely find the way to cast that works for you."

In your palm, you swear you can make out a slight cottony glow and gentle extra warmth. "*Fiat Lux!*" you whisper.

YOU FAIL IF X IS LESS THAN 9:

Shivers of fear overwhelm you. It's like you can feel the monsters again, lurking just outside the door, sniffing for blood, salivating for flesh. The glow in your hands dims to a pinpoint.

"How did the spellship look when it swooped in?" Mage Greene asks gently, "when the airmen landed to rescue you?"

"The ship was huge," you reply, "with lots of search lights." Just recalling it puts a smile on your face.

"Go on, details," the mage exhorts. "Magic's in the details."

"It had windows, uh... portholes," you correct yourself, "and when it touched down like a crow landing, the back opened up like a giant butt..." You chuckle. "...and our whole farm lit up like daytime."

"It was like the sun, yes?" the mage asks.

"Yeah, and the fiends screamed and flew off."

"Fantastic," the mage says. "Now focus on that spellship."

YOU LOSE 1 VITALITY POWERING THE LIGHT SPELL.

YOU MUST TRY AGAIN TO CAST THE SPELL. KEEP REPEATING THIS SECTION UNTIL YOU SUCCEED.

WHEN YOU SUCCEED:

A small, quiet luminous ball, first like a night-light and then like a lamplight, expands to highlight the soft folds in your child-sized hand. By a mere wish in your mind, the ball rises to brilliantly illuminate the whole room.

"Haaaa!" you gasp, and gawk.

Mage Greene smiles. "Good work, airman," he says, congratulating you like the base commander talking to his men.

By wiggling your fingers, the light dances.

You both laugh.

You wake up a tad fatigued.

Now, you're twenty-two years old, all grown up.

You're snug under the covers, eyes closed. As the dream slowly evaporates, Mage Greene's scraggly face sits like a big portrait in your sleepy mind's eye, a moment frozen in time.

Tick, tick, tick. Your "suite" is silent except for the alarm clock. It's big hand hasn't even touched six. It's still dark out.

You're damp with sweat. Tears sit imminent in your eyes, as if sad about something once found or soon lost.

You muse, *what an odd dream.* It was a crystal-clear memory from a decade ago. On that day, you'd been on base for a few years after being rescued, and Mage Greene believed you might have a gift for magic. If it weren't for his guidance, you wouldn't be the Special Lieutenant that you are now.

Okay, Lientenant, you say to yourself, urging your frame from the cot. You *could* go back to sleep or lounge in bed devouring a few more pages of a comic book. After all, you don't need to report for duty until 0730 hours. Or you could... *make yourself useful, Airman.*

You bumble out of bed and give yourself a sponge bath in your private loo—what a luxury! The magically gifted enjoy some extra amenities even in these tough times.

You brush your teeth and comb your ginger hair. You feel wariness as you inspect yourself in the mirror. *Yes, inspect yourself, Inspector.* That's your job on base, after all.

A wisp of intense fear briefly casts a shadow over your thoughts. There's a reason you still sleep with a night-light. But you shake off the shadow and head out. How about the shooting range? You can use this time to improve your firearm skills for that big mission that the Air Force hasn't assigned you yet.

GO TO THE NEXT SCENE.

Scene #2

Firing Range

It's still early, 0600 hours and just after dawn. You're at the base's firing range wearing ear and eye protection and a vest. You brought your favorite firearm, a shotgun you named Red Silver for its burnished copper and silver trim.

Bang! Woosh! You hit your target in the second of six concentric rings. It's a straw wheel some 30 yards away with a hobgoblin's big orange face pinned on it.

Bang! Woosh! You only hit the third ring. Maybe if you'd slept better, you'd have keener aim this morning.

"Nice shooting, C!" shouts your fellow officer, Special Lt. Slacks, as he saunters in. He and most of the guys call you "C" rather than "Airman Ernest". His voice is friendly but his face says sarcasm.

"She can give quite a percussive kick!" you shout back. Perhaps he'll get your hint and leave you to your thoughts.

"You're always up early," he says, "Getting the worm..."

You shrug. You prefer to exercise or enjoy a quiet walk before the day's hubbub starts and you get to work. But with the morning fog, drizzle, chill, and surprise bursts of rain, it felt best to check off the week's required target practice instead.

"I hope the rain will clear up later," you reply.

Mancy waltzes in. She's new to the base as an *ergo* specialist. Women on base are uncommon, and one with a knack for repairing and wrangling robots even rarer.

"Hey!" she shouts. You and Slacks doff your earmuffs. "How about we three put down a few coins?" She offers a challenge. "Let's start the day off with a bang."

"Sure thing," Slacks replies. Referring to your targets, he adds, "C here has the market cornered on coming in third."

You hesitate.

"Unless..." Slacks starts.

You interrupt. "Only if we do the gauntlet, with shotguns."

"You and that shotgun," Slacks groans. Typically on duty you all would use a pistol, but you're fond of Red Silver.

"Then it's sorted," Mancy replies. "Loser buys us all the good stuff." She means the freshly-brewed coffee you all normally have to pay for in the commissary.

You wonder, did you agree in order to save face, please Mancy, show up Slacks, or…? *Well, Nine Hells, now you've gotten yourself into this*, you tell yourself!

You three load shotguns with six shells each and line up each three yards apart. Mancy presses the big red "Go" button that runs the targets through an electro-mechanical gauntlet for 2 minutes that includes pop up civilians and other challenges.

Chug. Chug. Chug. The gauntlet starts.

HOW DO YOU PREPARE YOURSELF?
DO YOU 1) UTTER A PRAYER, 2) VISUALIZE
WINNING, 3) INSULT SLACKS, OR 4) GIVE MANCY
SOME GRIEF ABOUT "SHOOTING LIKE A LITTLE GIRL"?

You three start firing into the moving cavalcade of targets, aiming to hit the bulls-eye on the hobgoblin targets while avoiding everything else. During the Great War, hobgoblins were your nation's vicious foes.

TRY AN ACT OF AGILITY.
(X=D20. ADD +3 IF AGILITY IS A GIFT.
ADD +2 IF YOU VISUALIZE WINNING.
APPLY -5 IF YOU GAVE MANCY GRIEF.)

OPTION: DURING THE CONTEST, YOU CAN CAST AN
AIMING SPELL. THIS SIMPLE MAGIC MAKES IT EASIER
TO HIT YOUR NEXT TARGET. IF SO, SPEND 1 VITALITY
POINT NOW TO ADD +2 MORE TO YOUR D20 ROLL.

You fail if X is less than 12:

Ugh. Your aim is awful this morning. At this rate, you'll be court marshaled for excessive collateral damage. Meanwhile, Slacks and Mancy are neck and neck.

While you don't suffer any physical damage, coming in last is going to cost you in coins and reputation. To use Slacks' rich vocabulary, he can be an arse when he's not a brown-noser.

Roll again. You may spend 1 vitality to apply a +2 bonus from a spell, as before. If you get 12+, you beat Slacks but not Mancy and rank 2nd. If you get 17+ you beat Mancy too and rank 1st. Otherwise, you rank 3rd.

When you succeed:

Sometimes success means the challenge is over regardless of how you performed. And you keep in mind, this was just practice. It's not like any could have lost a limb of their lives, or even an eye for that matter, much less miss an armed enemy.

If you came in 3rd, you lose 2 coins. Otherwise, you get a free premium coffee. If you came in 1st, Slacks and Mancy give you respect and you gain one boon that you can use to gain a +5 bonus to any 1 roll later in the game.

Now in the commisary as you sit with a comic and enjoy some freshly brewed coffee, the base klaxons blare. *BWAAAHP!*

Moments later, your radio pager rings. Whatever the emergency, it has your name on it!

Go to the next scene.

Scene #3

Lead the Way

You stand on the tarmac with steaming coffee in hand. It's 0730. You pull up your bomber jacket hood against the gray drizzle, blustery wind, and flurries of swirling snow. Before you stands the Redkite, a sleek spellship. It has unexpectedly returned to base, and no one has emerged from it or responds to radio calls. You and others await the arrival of the base commander.

"What's happened?" you ask one of the ground crew.

"She returned to us a ghost ship."

"They're all dead, I bet" another adds. "Or sky-napped."

You spot no breaches or signs of damage to the spellship. All 22 yards of its steel torso gleam even in the rain.

"Or maybe they all bailed out," a third adds sarcastically, "after hearing what was for lunch." You're not sure if this guy was referring to Nessie, a mythical giant flying octopus that lurks in the clouds and hunts in the nearby mountains, or to the Air Force's infamous cardboard-like meals in winter.

You look around. Mage Greene is not about. Surely he'd be one of the first on this mystery?

"He was on the ship," an airman replies when you ask.

Oh no! You dare not imagine what's befallen him, and without him or the ship's pilot, you and Slacks are among the few airmen here who are magically adept. Surely one of you will lead the investigation. You consider, if Mage Greene were here, what would he do?

Look and listen, he would say. *Ask questions.*

"Anyone look in the windows?" you ask, wanting details.

"They're covered in dust from the inside" Slacks answers, coming up behind you. "The guys say that Redkite here took off on a routine personnel and equipment transfer to Fort Braggart." That's an hour's flight away. "But eighteen minutes

16

later, she returned to base."

"How'd it land?" you ask, incredulous. Who or what turned the ship around? Your brain is already at work. A spell-ship requires a magically gifted pilot strapped into its *spellhelm*. Without the pilot, it can't navigate or land on its own.

"No idea, yet," Slacks replies.

"Mage Greene was on board," you say, a little shaken. Slacks has known the mage only since arriving here a few months ago, whereas you've known the mage for years. The mage has been training you two together.

"Yeah," Slacks replies stoically. "So one of us will have to man up and take charge of this mission, get inside that bird. Seniority has its perks."

"We can only hope," you reply sarcastically. Technically, Slacks has been a Special Lieutenant longer than you have and has more experience, but you are definitely more spell-wise.

From a nearby door, the base commander, Hollingsworth, plus his staff sergeant and an unfamiliar male civilian exit and head your way.

You see Slacks has in hand a file on the ship, presumably including its schematics and cargo and crew complement.

"Opportunities come to those who are on the ball," he brags to you. He gives you a competitive wink. You doubt he has had to time to study the file.

"Good, you two are already here," the Commander says. "This warrants immediate investigation. We can call in outside help, but let's figure out what's happened first and take care of any mess. By the book, that gives us 48 hours."

"I'm already on it, sir," Slacks tells him.

"I see." The Commander notes the folder with approval.

HOW DO YOU MAKE YOUR CASE TO LEAD?
DO YOU EMPHASIZE YOUR 1) COOL HEADEDNESS,
2) MAGICAL TALENT, 3) YEARS ON THE BASE, OR 4)
CLOSENESS WITH THE MISSING MAGE?

As you start to make your case to lead the mission, the Commander adds, "Oh, this is Mr. Calv Nyquist," referring to the civilian. "His crate of *cake* is on this bird." Cake means Top Secret stuff. You wonder, Calv is a common name in your homeland and his features look like folks there. Is he a refugee like you from the Great War?

"Airmen," Calv says confidently, giving you and Slacks both piercing eye contact and firm handshakes.

"Special Lieutenants Ernest and Slacks," the Commander says. "They are fine, gifted investigators."

Now is your chance to lead the investigation. You straighten your shoulders and make your case.

TRY AN ACT OF CHARM.
(X=D20. ADD +3 IF CHARM IS A GIFT. ADD +2 IF YOU EMPHASIZE YOUR COOL HEADEDNESS.)

YOU FAIL IF X IS LESS THAN 14:

As you make your case to lead the mission, Calv interrupts. "Aren't you a little young?" he asks you as if testing your confidence. "I've got expensive gear in there."

He's sort of right. You completed Command School a year ago. But while you are a newly minted lieutenant, you also classify as "Special", as in you wield magic. That's rare in the Commonweal and almost everywhere else in the world. The odds are maybe one in two hundred unless someone's a ginger like you.

You reply, "I grew up here on the base and have been around spellships most of my life. I can take the pilot's seat on Redkite and give you a full tour of its capabilities if you like."

Calv smiles widely. "I may take you up on your offer."

Turning his attention to the spellship, he takes several big paces toward it. "What are we waiting for?" he asks.

You consider. Calv is a variable, an unknown, oozing

with impatient confidence and likely unfamiliar with military protocol or true danger. But you like to accommodate.

"Mr. Nyquist," you reply, "I'll take Lt. Slacks here and check out this bird's innards and keep an open radio to you, and to the sergeant here." You look the sergeant's way.

"Got it," Calv replies.

Slacks glowers at you.

With your left hand in your trousers, you rub a tiny charm, ready if needed to cast a spell in your favor. Over the years, Mage Greene has shown you ways to use your gifts discretely.

YOU MUST ROLL AGAIN.
IF YOU SUCCEED, CONTINUE BELOW. OR IF YOU FAIL,
YOU EXPEND 1 VITALITY POINT TO POWER A CHARM
SPELL, WHICH GRANTS YOU THE EXTRA CHARM YOU
NEED, THEN CONTINUE BELOW.

WHEN YOU SUCCEED:

"Airman Ernest," the Commander says, meaning you, "you're on point for this."

"Yessir," you say, barely containing your excitement.

"And let's handle it internally, shall we," he adds. "Figure it all out before we report it."

"Right away, understood, sir." You haven't faced a mystery like this, but you aim to do your best.

"What else do we know?" you ask.

Slacks quickly responds. "ATC says the spellship reported itself at Paladin's Point in the mountains nine minutes after it took off. However, that point is usually fourteen minutes away."

"ATC?" Calv asks, not knowing the term.

"Air Traffic Control," Slacks explains.

"Hmm, very odd," you say, then you remember it's best to stay quiet and listen until more is known.

"I suggest you get into that bird straight away. Our men inside may be languishing."

"Yessir," you and Slacks reply.

Puzzling out the discrepancy in flight time, not to mention how the ship maybe landed on its own, will have to wait.

"Slacks, get us radios, some backup with rifles on the tarmac, and medics with stretchers."

"Sure thing, C," he replies informally. He gives you a look that you may pay for this later, then he runs off calling on others for what you asked.

Mancy appears, and he heads her way.

The Commander leans in and says in a hushed tone, "Airman Ernest, a promotion might be in this for you. Particularly since Slacks—what an apropos name—came to us with red marks on his last job."

"Understood, Sir". You didn't know this and wonder why the Commander mentions it now.

"Anything else I should know?" you ask.

"Calv has his box of goodies onboard," the Commander replies, "and Mage Greene was transporting his technocrat."

"Mad Muse?" you ask, confirming. *Mad Muse* was the name everyone gave to the mage's electromechanical technomagical contraption, ostensibly used for intelligence purposes.

"At fifty-thousand sterling each, those pieces are each worth as much as the ship." Considering you earn five sterling a day, you surmise it would take you over half a century to buy them even if you saved all of your money.

"I won't let you down, sir," you reply.

"Good. We've got it sorted then. I'll leave you to it."

You haven't faced such a challenging mystery before. During the past year, you've gotten used to small potatoes, trifles such as a ventriloquist hedgehog stalking the base. But here on the tarmac, a monstrous potato beckons.

GO TO THE NEXT SCENE.

PART II

BELLY OF
THE BIRD

Scene #4

Scanning Wand

At 0730 hours, you and Slacks prepare to enter Redkite, the oddly quiet spellship. Besides gloves and breathing filters, you need a zap gun, radio headsets, and a scanning wand.

The sergeant joins you with a red suitcase. He is hungover, perhaps after a long visit to his lady friend in town the night before. He unlocks the suitcase and hands it to you.

From it, you take its centerpiece, a scanning wand, while Slacks takes from it a red evidence bag and empty vials.

"You expecting a fight?" Calv asks, looking at the wand.

You explain. "Despite being called a wand, it's mundane electrotech that can detect and analyze life."

The wand fails to turn on even as you flip its switch a few times. "Likely dead batteries," you explain.

"Get us two fresh tinnies, quick like," Slacks calls to a nearby airman, who hustles off.

While you wait, the ground crew pulls up a flight of wheeled stairs to the spellship. The stairs are your ticket in.

The recruit returns. "Batteries, Lieutenant".

Annoyingly, even with fresh batteries, the wand is still dead. You know it's delicate, even temperamental. You sit on the stair steps and open up the wand to fix it. Besides batteries, there are two wires—red and blue—and a set of five crystals each attached to a gauge. The crystals are designed to resonate when they are electrically charged and adjacent to specific materials. Fortunately, no crystals are burned out, but the red wire is loose. Hopefully, it just needs rejiggering rather than resoldering. Working the minute components will require close work.

Try an Act of Agility.
(X=D20. Add +3 if Agility is a Gift.)

You fail if X is less than 9:

After donning a rubber glove from the suitcase and attaching a grounding wire, you tighten the red wire. You close the wand and flip its switch.

Nothing.

"How about we give Slacks a go at it," the sergeant says.

"Yeah, C, how about it?" Slacks replies. He smirks.

You suppress any hint of annoyance. Slacks isn't any better trained than you are with electrotech, which he knows, and you are not keen to promote him over yourself.

You reply, "No need. I've figured out what it is."

You re-open the wand and pretend to be busy as you whisper "*Exsarcio!*" under your breath. It's the simple *Mending* spell. You cross your fingers for luck.

You close the wand and keep your mouth shut as you flip the switch again.

Powering the Mending spell costs 1 vitality point. Continue to success.

When you succeed:

The wand hums to life.

"Good news gentlemen," you say, as you deftly wave the wand over Calv. It beeps. "You're alive! And a male human at that," you inform him.

Calv laughs.

"Will it also tell you my net worth?" he asks. Apparently, simply being alive is insufficient for Calv's ambitions.

"Only when you owe taxes," you answer back jovially.

You all have a morbid laugh.

Go to the next scene.

SCENE #5

CLOUD OF CLUES

It's time to enter and survey the spellship. Hopefully, there are answers and no nasty surprises. A bunch of corpses would provide an easy answer but the saddest scenario. In this case, you hope for a mystery.

You and Slacks climb the stairs to the spellship's airlock. It sports a helpful safety placard: "Warning: Hatch may open." Slacks unhinges and applies a bit of muscle to open it. He's definitely the stronger of you two.

You both climb in and quickly shut the hatch behind you to prevent escape of any creatures or contaminants or whatever else might itch to get out.

Inside it is dead still and dark except for ribbons of gray morning light coming through the narrow, dusty portholes.

"Wait," you whisper to Slacks as you stop. You take out a tiny packet. Into the palm of your hand, you empty its contents—less than a teaspoon of orange-colored salt crystals. You snort hard.

"Classy," Slacks says. "Real classy."

"That coffee hit me hard," you explain. Coffee, like tobacco, neutralizes spell dust, the element that bends the brain to make magic possible. "I didn't want to snort in public."

"Uh-huh," Slacks replies. "Or in front of Mancy?" She's joined the mission but waits outside with the others, holding the radio and keeping an eye on the stretchers and extra guns, if needed.

You make a quick gesture, with two fingers up like a light bulb's filament, and the other fingers folded in, and you wave that arm and speak the magic words, "Fiat Lux!" An orb of bright light appears in your palm. Just like you dreamed this morning, this was the first spell you ever learned, though you now cast it your own way.

With gentle thoughts and twinges of your index finger, you push the luminous orb up and around the ship's main cabin.

There are no visible bodies, blood, monsters, or even signs of disturbance, at least at first glance. You're certainly glad to not see Mage Greene's corpse.

There is an unnatural layer of pale dust everywhere. Normally, a ship would be spit-polish clean, especially a prized hybrid of electrotech and magic like Redkite.

"Samples," you direct Slacks.

"Yeah, yeah, already on it," he replies as he squats and carefully gathers some of the pale dust into a sample vial.

You leave the Lux orb hovering at the ceiling as you take photos with your favorite little box camera, which you named Snowflake for its stylish etching. It was a gift from the mage for your fifteenth birthday. He showed you how long to leave the camera's shutter open, among other adjustments, and the Lux's light makes it all simple.

"Take any nudes with that?" Slacks asks.

You answer seriously. "Sometimes I take Snowflake out into the woods, around town, or near the lake on sunny or foggy days to have some fun with her."

Slacks laughs. "Buddy, you're off your cob."

You take more photographs: *Snap, snap, snap* at forward, aft, and starboard; then s*nap, snap, snap* for port, ceiling, and floor.

"There are drops of blood here," Slacks reports as he takes samples from around the spellhelm in the ship's cockpit.

You go over and *snap, snap, snap* with your camera.

"How much blood?" Mancy asks over the radio. You'd almost forgotten about the folks outside.

"A half-dozen drops," Slacks answers.

"Anything else?" you ask, peering around.

"The ergo," Slacks says, pointing starboard.

The ship's ergo—a hulking worker robot—stands rigidly

and silently in its cubby at the ship's starboard midsection. It's a simple-minded workhorse.

"Can you question it?" Calv asks them over the radio.

"No can do," Mancy replies in the background.

Slacks quickly reports: "I was here yesterday when Mage Greene tasked the ergo to move his Mad Muse onto the ship. Let me tell you, it weighs a ton. Then we shut it off."

Mancy adds, "The ergo's simple. No memory anyway."

You further explain to Calv, "Ergos are normally shut off during flight unless emergency repairs are needed or the ship is about to be boarded, and..."

"No wait...." You stop mid-sentence. Something feels off to you. Time to investigate the ergo more closely.

Upon closer inspection, you spot a set of tracks through the dust—ergo tracks—leading from its cubby to the pilot seat and then back.

What do you see, Special Lieutenant?" the Sergeant asks.

"The ergo is shut down but its tracks lead to and from the spellhelm."

WHERE DO YOU FOCUS YOUR ATTENTION?
1) THE ERGO, 2) THE SPELLHELM, 3) THE PATH
BETWEEN THE TWO, OR 4) ELSEWHERE NEARBY.

You inspect the controls in front of the spellhelm. The console is intact. You know it fairly well. You've had basic pilot training plus a dozen hours in this majestic puppy on account of your magical blood. After all, the Air Force is all about flying, and what little kid grows up on an airbase and doesn't dream of taking the pilot's seat?

TRY AN ACT OF INTELLECT.
(X=D20. ADD +3 IF INTELLECT IS A GIFT.
ADD +2 IF YOU FOCUSED ON THE SPELLHELM.)

YOU FAIL IF X IS LESS THAN 12:

You don't see how the evidence connects. Maybe there aren't enough puzzle pieces yet to figure things out?

You don't recall how to manually print the ship's log tape.

"*Manum inconspicuam!*" you utter under your breath. It's a spell to briefly activate a machine without touching it.

The gauges and meters activate briefly, flashing recent settings. Importantly, the helm spits out a few feet of log tape.

POWERING THE ACTIVATE SPELL COSTS 1 VITALITY POINT. CONTINUE TO SUCCESS.

WHEN YOU SUCCEED:

"Got the log," you report as you pull out the log tape.

The tape records changes of course and other helm actions with time stamps. At a minimum, it records "Normal" at one minute intervals. As you closely examine the tape, you spot two gaps, each 5 minutes long. The tape also shows that the helm pivoted the spellship to return to base. Everything else is "Normal." But who manned the spellhelm to land?

"There's a ten-minute gap," you tell everyone. "It's as if the helm was briefly shut off or it simply skipped ahead in time."

You look out through the helm's dusty glass. Down on the tarmac, the flight crew along with Calv, Mancy, and the sergeant are huddled around the radio listening to you explain.

"You see my crate yet?" Calv asks.

You do. Some ten yards away to the rear, it's strapped in securely for flight, intact with a fine layer of dust on it.

"It's fine," Slacks replies.

You two head over to examine it.

GO TO THE NEXT SCENE.

Scene #6
Ergo Gone Wild

"Ahh!" Slacks yells in agony as he drops to the ground. The ergo lumbers forward.

You back up and reach for your shotgun, but little help that will be against a steel-man with no blood or guts. It is a 9-foot-tall windmill of metal and wood. You've seen one easily lift a half-ton over its head and pull a spellship on the tarmac. One arm ends in a set of fine grippers akin to fingers and thumbs, while the other ends in a large hammer and wrench system.

As Slacks struggles to rise, the ergo bashes him again using its hammer. "Agh!" He cries as he falls to the ground with a splatter of blood. Slacks moans and closes his eyes, unconscious.

The ergo moves methodically toward you.

"Stop!" you command it.

It continues forward.

"Halt!" you shout in Mechan, the robot language. No luck.

It closes in and raises its hammer arm.

How do you plan to fend off the ergo?
1) Shoot it, 2) Punch it, 3) Taser it,
4) Push it away, or 5) Run and hide?

Whatever you're thinking, the ergo is already upon you! You grapple it, figuring that it's not trained for combat, and if you're on it, it'll be too close to just slam you.

Try an Act of Brawn.
(X=D20. Add +3 if Brawn is a gift.
Add +2 if you used your zap gun.)

————————————————

You fail if X is less than 10:

The ergo is awkward but its servos are incredibly strong! Worse, it's plainly trying to pin you so it can bash your skull as if driven by hatred.

You call down your Lex orb into its face, momentarily blinding it while you grab for your zap gun.

Gun in hand, you fire. *Zzzzzt*, you electrocute it.

The ergo jerks wildly. For a moment you fear it will crush you but it loosens its grip.

YOU LOSE 1D6 VITALITY POINTS.
YOU MUST KEEP TRYING UNTIL YOU SUCCEED.

WHEN YOU SUCCEED:

The ergo collapses, inanimate. *Whew!*

"Mates?" Mancy yells over the radio. "You okay?"

"Report lieutenants!" the sergeant shouts.

"Slacks here," he reports, slowly standing while steadying himself on the bulkhead. He finds blood as he checks his shoulder with a leery eye. "Frick the gods!" he exclaims as he gently pokes at his battered shoulder. "C's a little disoriented.'"

"I'm fine," you correct as you roll out from under the ergo.

"You sure it was shut off?" Mancy asks from afar.

"Yeah," you reply. "It just went wild."

"Savage bastard had it out for us, with intent to kill," Slacks adds. "I saw bloodlust in its eyes."

"That can't be," Mancy explains. "Unless..."

"Magic?" the sergeant asks.

"Or a ghost, or a remote control, or..." Mancy begins with honest enthusiasm and excitement.

"You need support?" the sergeant asks.

"No, sir," you and Slacks say in unison. "All men up."

"The answers lie with further investigation," you add.

GO TO THE NEXT SCENE.

SCENE #7

MAD MUSE

"Let's look at this 'Mad Muse,'" you say. The big machine's name tickles your funny bone. It reminds you of the colorful naked stone pixies on the base's front lawn, which all the airmen call "the rear guard."

The machine is a wonder of modern electrotech. You look it over and report: "Mad Muse here is a metal cube, maybe five feet per side. Transport tag says it's 500 pounds. It has caster wheels. Those are locked. There are lights on top, presently off. Hundreds of labeled buttons adorn its chassis."

You peer at the buttons. Their labels include names of creatures, deities, devices, historical events, medical procedures, nations, personages, places, realms of existence, recipes, spells, and more. They are organized with a librarian's exactitude.

A few times, you've watched Mage Greene using it. He once explained, inside is a phonographic recording for each button. You press a button to load and play its record. A record runs for twelve minutes. The attached trumpet acts as the speaker. It also sports a crank, though the machine is electrical, and you've never seen that in use.

You can't miss its front. It sports a devilish mechanical face with a waist-high open maw. It's creepy, like someone's idea of a bad joke.

"It doesn't bite," Slacks advises. He chuckles sadistically.

You give him a hard stare.

Mancy asks, "What was its last query?"

"Good question," you reply. Normally, the mouth spits out paper tape from a spool, offering written copy, text or diagrams. You peer up into the maw and spot an edge of torn paper but nothing more. "No clue," you reply.

You wave the scanning wand over Mad Muse.

"Beep!" the wand immediately responds back.

The wand's five gauges go wild, then quickly settle down.

"You've got the touch," Slacks remarks. "Maybe it's another gopher?" he jokes. You spent much of last week chasing a gopher on the base, one that someone—from the spell lab, or elsewhere—enchanted so the poor varmint emitted cries of distress with a young lady's voice. Perhaps it was meant as a practical joke for your birthday, also last week? None of your mates have fessed up to it yet. Now that you think about it, Slacks surely had a hand. Maybe he knows a ventriloquism spell? He plays his magic close to his vest.

"Mad Muse is... alive!" you slowly report, surprised.

"What?!" the sergeant says. Normally, a machine doesn't radiate life. Even if it carries some spell enchantment, it's still just a bundle of disks, gears, wires, and whatnot.

"Weird," Slacks adds.

"Not good," Mancy says. Unfortunately, her word is probably the closest to the truth.

You get into details. "The gauges say cloth, metal, and wood in abundance, as expected, but also too much fluid, and flesh, though those two gauges are swinging up and down." You tap the wand a few times, then turn it off and on to reset it, in case it's simply malfunctioning. It gives the same weird result.

"It's as if... at one moment some creature's there and the next moment it's not."

The seat by Mad Muse is dust-free, in a butt-shaped pattern. Likely Mage Greene was sitting in that seat.

"Looky here," Slacks adds, pointing to tiny drops of blood—a gentle splatter—near Mad Muse and the wizard's seat.

You report this over the radio, then squat down to get a better look at this contraption.

WHAT'S YOUR APPROACH?
DO YOU 1) ANALYZE ITS MAGICAL AURA, 2) TURN IT ON AND WORK ITS BUTTONS, 3) STUDY ITS DESIGN, OR 4) TRY TO COMMUNICATE WITH IT?

"Hello?" Slacks says to the machine. "Anyone in there?"

You both listen, not sure what you might hear.

Silence.

A shiver runs up your spine as if a ghost is passing through you or touching you in response.

You two spend a few more minutes fiddling with it, visually studying its design.

"Sarge," Slacks radios, "We can turn it on, try to work it."

"Don't advise, but it's your call, Lieutenants."

Slacks looks at you and whispers away from the radio: "Got your zap gun handy?"

"This machine can't assault us," you point out, "and its worth more than our salaries for a lifetime. Let's proceed with deliberate caution. I have an idea."

"What kind of magic is it?" Calv asks from over the radio. "Maybe it's ensorcelled in some way?"

Good question. You stand back and rub an amulet around your neck. "*Fateor*," you whisper. The charm was a gift upon graduating from Command School. It causes any and all magical items or such within fifteen feet to glow.

TRY AN ACT OF INTELLECT.
(X=D20. ADD +3 IF INTELLECT IS A GIFT.
ADD +2 IF YOU ANALYZE ITS MAGICAL AURA.)

IF X IS GREATER THAN 10,
YOU LEARN THIS NEW INFORMATION:

The charm glows. Of nine possible colors, it glows amber and gray. You report, "I'm getting it accesses supernatural knowledge beyond its mechanical disks. And it's uh... conjuring something"

"Conjuring what?" Mancy asks from over the radio.

"The aura's strong," Slacks observes, peering at your

charm. He whispers to you: "Like I said, a gopher's in there."

"Hmm." You know a dozen basic spells and one or two more interesting ones, but theory of magic is far beyond your training. Generally, magic that summons creatures is forbidden, but it could be summoning a phenomenon such as light or sound. Or maybe Mad Muse is possessed like the ergo was or otherwise holding a random residual charge of magical energy? You make a mental note for later to investigate this question.

USING THE AMULET COSTS 1 VITALITY POINT.
CONTINUE BELOW.

"Just look inside," Mancy encourages.

You don't really like that idea. You wouldn't call yourself a yellow belly, but you certainly prefer to not stick your hand or face into anything electromechanical or techno-magical that might go rogue.

"Yeah, Special Lieutenant, take a look," Slacks teases you in a hushed voice. He takes out his zap gun and unlocks the safety. "I'm ready this time without hesitation to shoot the crap out of whatever's inside, the moment it moves."

"We're standing by to support you," the sergeant says.

"Yes, take a look inside," Calv urges. Not that a civilian's desires matter much to you.

You have an uneasy feeling about poking around. What do you do?

YOU LOSE 1 SANITY POINT IF YOU ANALYZED
ITS MAGICAL AURA. YOU LOSE 2 SANITY POINTS IF
YOU TRIED TO COMMUNICATE WITH IT.

NOW, IF YOU OPEN "MAD MUSE",
GO TO THE NEXT SCENE.
OTHERWISE, GO TO SCENE #9 (PAGE 36).

Scene #8

Inside Mad Muse

You decide to get a look inside Mage Greene's techno-magical contraption, Mad Muse. Everyone else is eager to know what cute, disgusting, or bizarre creature lurks inside, if any, and you aim to please. You sigh and kneel to carefully open the technocrat's back panel.

"Opening it up," you report over the radio. You wait and listen while silently counting to ten. It's turned off so you shouldn't hear anything. *Good: no noises.*

You peer in.

Inside, its innards look "normal" with wires and disks. That is, nothing is moving, shorting, flittering, or oozing. But what do you know beyond a semester of Elementary Electrotech? Only Mancy or a lab tech could really know.

"Lighting it up," you report. Mentally, and with your index finger, your call down your Lux orb from the ceiling to thread its way into the machine and glow up its innards. The orb floats over, illuminating everything as it goes.

In places, there is a pale purplish glow.

"There's energy," you report.

Whether it's merely electrical from its batteries or magical from something or someone else, you can't tell.

TRY AN ACT OF AGILITY.
(X=D20. ADD +3 IF AGILITY IS A GIFT.)

YOU FAIL IF X IS LESS THAN 10:

Pzzzzzt! An electrical arc hits you in the face. "Agh!" you shout. It's not bad, but it stings.

You feel wretchedly nauseous as if you're going to puke. Thankfully, your stomach already digested your tiny breakfast.

YOU LOSE 1 VITALITY AND 1D3 SANITY POINTS. CONTINUE TO SUCCESS.

WHEN YOU SUCCEED:

"Ah ha!" You spy a six-inch diameter geometric pattern—a sigil—inked on a small plate in glistening red paint. Or maybe it's wet blood? The sigil is unfamiliar. It is somewhat like the sigils of various gods from olden times, but different. Just looking at it makes you feel ill.

Wait… you know this feeling. Your mind rewinds. As a kid when devils came, they sniffed out mortals, no matter their hiding place, and merely touching their gear or getting close to them invoked nausea. This here now is the feeling of Hell.

"You got this, C?" Slacks asks.

"Yeah, I'm okay."

Snap, snap. You slowly take some photos. Besides the photos, you also visually memorize the sigil. Your head is good at detail like this, and you of all people will remember this.

"Slacks," give me a sample vial to get some of this paint or blood, and I'll…."

Before your eyes, the sigil fades. No trace of it remains.

"Dognabbit!" you exclaim. That's the closest you get to cursing. You take up the wand again. "Life readings are now zero," you report. "Whatever it was is gone."

"Gods damn," Slacks replies.

Something fiendish definitely touched this ship, but you decide to keep this little insight to yourself for the moment.

YOU GAIN A +5 BONUS TO YOUR ROLL IN SCENE #10. GO TO THE NEXT SCENE.

Scene #9

We All Fall Down

You and Slacks are nearly ready to wrap up. But first, you need to investigate the spellship's aft section, which has Calv's crate and the seats where most of the missing airmen sat. What's in that crate, and is it also possessed by some strange, nauseating energy?

If you had an option, you would disembark now and continue your investigation from a safe distance. A feeling of dread pervades the back of the ship. Alas, duty—orders and others' expectations—compel you to continue. You sigh.

"What of my crate?" Calv asks impatiently over the radio.

You and Slacks slowly walk over to it. Neither of you is excited to get smashed or burnt again. It is likely specialized electrotech licensed to the military by Calv's company.

How do you prepare yourself?
Do you 1) Utter a prayer, 2) Ready your zap gun, 3) Prepare a Shield spell, 4) Let Slacks go ahead without you, or 5) Do nothing special?

You two head to the back of the ship. Slacks gets to the crate first, and while you two contemplate how to deal with it, waves of nausea briefly wash over you again.

You wave the wand over the crate. It indicates no life or anything else, actually. You notice the crate sports lead seals.

"The wand can't say. The crate's lead-lined," you report.

"Yes, Lieutenants," Calv replies. "It's harmless."

You wonder by whose authority it is officially "harmless." Your vision narrows and you feel shaky.

The sergeant suggests, "Just make sure it's intact."

"That it is," Slacks says.

Another wave of nausea bludgeons you. Is there a devil

here? You begin to shake. You vaguely see Slacks clutching his stomach and possibly burping up something. Or is that you, viewing yourself out of your body?

"Report," the sergeant or maybe Calv requests.

"C?!" Slacks grabs your arm in alarm.

Everything briefly goes dark. You cry out for help, whether that's aloud or silently, you can't tell.

TRY AN ACT OF ENDURANCE.
(X=D20. ADD +3 IF ENDURANCE IS A GIFT.
ADD +2 IF YOU UTTERED A PRAYER.)

YOU FAIL IF X IS LESS THAN 14:

You're somewhere, crying and young.

Your mother is scolding you in the kitchen. You're six years old. Warm autumn light streams through the windows and the aroma of mincemeat pie wafts from the stove.

"What in the world possessed you?" she barks, "to steal flowers from the Postners' garden?"

"But I picked them for you!" you blurt from under tears.

"No excuse, none at all, thievery is not in our blood," she retorts. "Just wait until your father gets home!"

You receive no supper, and you scamper into the attic, shivering as night falls, to avoid your father's wrath.

Later, there are screams... and chirping, mewling, and yawling of fiends. Screams. Your heart skips a few beats...

You awaken, gasping for air.

You're back on the cold metal deck of the Redkite, curled up like a little kid. You taste vomit.

"Frick!" Slacks exclaims, kneeling by you, concerned.

"Report, Lieutenants," you hear over the radio. You honestly can't tell if that's the sergeant, Mancy or someone else.

"Fine here," Slacks replies. "C just tripped. Freaky bird."

"Okay," sergeant replies. "Perhaps it's time to finish up." You appreciate sergeant's care.

"Thanks, mate," you tell Slacks as he helps you up. He is showing his true stripes.

"Yeah." He looks a little pale, and adds with a whisper, "You were shaking hard but I didn't see anything."

YOU LOSE 1D6 SANITY POINTS.
CONTINUE TO SUCCESS.

WHEN YOU SUCCEED:

Feeling better, you two finish up. The seats where the twelve missing airmen sat are dust-free. Like the wizard's seat up front, each of the twelve sports a butt-shaped, dust-free pattern. *Whew!* At least the dust isn't mortal remains! That means maybe the airmen and Mage Greene and the flight crew are alive somewhere? Above the seats, the airmen's duffle bags are still in their rigging and covered in fine dust.

"No signs of our men," Slacks reports, "But we got ourselves twelve butt shadows with gear."

Where did the dust come from? you wonder.

"Any blood?" Calv asks.

"Not a bit," you reply, though you're not really looking.

"Good," Mancy says. "I'll ready some airmen to retrieve the ergo and anything else, unless you advise they stay put."

"Stay put for now," you decide.

"What's your conclusion, sprouts?" the sergeant asks. *Sprouts?* You wonder. That's rather presumptuous. Even though he's two decades older than you and Slacks, he's not an officer.

"We're at the epicenter," Slacks reflects.

You add, "with only more questions."

GO TO THE NEXT SCENE.

PART III

MIRROR, MIRROR

Scene #10

Private Matters

It's 1030 hours. You rifle through Mage Greene's office—his desk, shelves, and drawers—in search of clues. It feels a little inappropriate as you get acquainted with his private matters.

His secretary Alba let you into his space. You spent many hours over the years in the adjacent laboratory but not here in his cramped office. Fortunately, Alba knows the password to get past the door without triggering a ward against intruders. After all, someone had to clean the room on occasion.

Straight away, on the mage's desk, a grainy photo of him and you as a young man confronts you. You smile. In those years, you had some tough challenges and got into trouble more than once, mainly for thieving snacks, comic books, and minor artist tools from the commissary.

"Will anyone be joining you?" Alba asks. You imagine she is planning how many tea cups to prepare.

"Just me this morning," you reply.

"Very good, Sir," she says, hiding her worry, and vanishes back to her own nook on the far side of the laboratory.

Presently, as leader in solving this mystery, you've assigned Slacks to develop the photos you took and analyze the dust samples he collected. Mancy will examine the ergo and Mad Muse, but at your request, she's now with the sergeant and a squad to search for the missing airmen, likely near Paladin's Peak. She's sharp and will surely find them.

You scan the shelves. Numerous books line them, but none are spell books or address the occult.

You find a packet of aged photos of a young Mage Greene in a more carefree time with his wife and children. He lost them to a bombing raid during the Great War. For any magic user at that time, starting a family invited trouble. Was magic heritable? Should people of different ancestry intermarry? Moreover, his wife was human and he a goliath. Recent laws of freedom in parliament resolved those questions in a liberal way, but the mage grew up in a paranoid era.

To my dearest Wise Wolf on your birthday, the back of one photo reads, presumably written to him by his wife.

You wonder what it is like to have loved and lost.

"Finding everything you need?" Alba asks as she brings you a steaming cup of tea.

"Yes, Alba."

"Good to hear," she replies. She was a civilian who had worked on base since the age of sixteen. She never married though Mage Greene did quietly comment once that she enjoyed a dalliance with an airmen who later died in an airfight.

"Thank you for the tea," you say after you take a nice long sip to rejuvenate yourself. "Did he perhaps have a safe?"

"I believe so." She leads you to a high cupboard. Within is an iron box, placed up high befitting a man who stood a good two feet above everyone else. Even Slacks looks short beside him. "I'm sorry to say, I don't know of any way into it."

"Magic no doubt," you reply. "I'll figure it out." Surely, he had a plan in case of his untimely demise.

HOW DO YOU DEAL WITH THE SAFE?
YOU FOCUS ON FINDING 1) THE RIGHT COMBINA-
TION, 2) MAGICAL WARDS, 3), AN ALTERNATE MODE
TO GET IN, OR 4) BREAKING OPEN THE SAFE?

Standing on a chair, you examine the safe carefully. It is made of iron with lead clasps to disguise the presence of any magic within. Mechanically, it relies on a combination lock requiring the correct dialing of three numbers. *Hmm, what are the three digits?* And does it have a magical layer of protection?

TRY AN ACT OF INTELLECT.
(X=D20 + 3 IF INTELLECT IS A GIFT. ADD +3 IF YOU
FOCUS ON FINDING THE RIGHT COMBINATION.)

OPTION: YOU CAN CAST A SHIELD SPELL.
THIS COSTS 1 VITALITY POINT NOW AND WILL
REDUCE ANY DAMAGE YOU MIGHT POSSIBLY SUFFER.

YOU FAIL IF X IS LESS THAN 15:

You try several numeric combinations such as the mage's birthday, your birthday, and even the "lucky numbers" on a slip birthed by a broken fortune cookie on his desk.

Zzzz! After the third failed attempt, a blast of electricity knocks you across the room against a bookshelf. Since you were standing on a chair, you take a hard knock to the head.

"Ugh," you blurt as you struggle to stay conscious.

Alba rushes in. "Oh no! You alright?" she cries with great concern.

"Yes, yes, thank you."

"Airmen always say that. Just stay down until you get your bearings and let me check you for bleeding."

Good news: You suffer from minor bleeding, and after a few minutes you are sitting up, more clear-headed and comfortable as she refills your tea.

YOU LOSE 3D6 VITALITY, OR ONLY 1D6 VITALITY
IF YOU CAST THE PROTECTION SPELL EARLIER.
CONTINUE TO SUCCESS.

WHEN YOU SUCCEED:

You hunt around the office. What would the mage do? How would he think? He was often absent-minded and reserved, sometimes painfully so, but he had a soft spot for people he really liked. You take hold of the photo of you and Mage Greene. That was the day he adopted you officially. You open up the back of the photo case and find three digits recording the date, the 14th of February, 1927. You try that.

Turn, turn, *click*. Turn, *click*. Turn, *click*.

You open the safe!

Indeed, it is stuffed with notebooks and personal items, some of which might be magical.

You unload its contents onto the desk and a nearby stool. There are three notebooks, a spellbook, a few other books of magic, an oak wand inscribed with the elvish word for healing, a pouch of gold coins, and a pair of matching diamond wedding rings. You expected there would be vials of spell dust, but there's none. Many of the latter items like the rings are plainly not relevant to the case, though a dour thought crosses your mind, that you are the mage's sole heir.

A slip of paper pops out. It reads, *Dear Airman Ernest, if you find this note, take what you need.—Greene*

You sit at the desk. Plainly, it was built especially for the mage's tall frame and you resort to standing and stooping.

"Success?" Alba asks as she comes in.

"Happily, the clues were meant for me."

"Of course." She gives a sweet wink. "You have earned your wings."

You laugh lightly. "So I have."

"And how do you judge the situation? Will we be seeing our dear Mage Greene again soon?"

Hmm, you wonder. In your heart, you feel you will. But something dark and heavy also lurks there. "I hope so, Alba, I hope so."

YOU GAIN A HEALING WAND WORTH 300 COINS. IT HAS 3 USES LEFT. EACH USE HEALS 5 VITALITY. THE OTHER PERSONAL EFFECTS SUCH AS WEDDING RINGS ARE LIKELY WORTH A BIT, BUT YOU LEAVE THEM BE, LOVELY AS THEY ARE.

GO TO THE NEXT SCENE.

Scene #11

Three Big Clues

Looking through Mage Greene's private books and note-books, you focus on finding anything that looks fresh or recent. Alas, he wasn't one for writing dates.

Try an Act of Intellect.
(X=D20 + 3 if Intellect is a gift. Add +5 if you completed Scene #8, looking inside mad muse.)

You fail if X is less than 17:

You waste a bit of time reading, unsure what's important. You find a summoning spell, but it doesn't cause the summoner or an object to be possessed. That's not a match!

There is a small, brown-leather clad book on time travel, or at least the philosophy thereof… wait, actually, it offers fascinating sections. It includes a treatise with diagrams by a mesmerist named Dr. Theodore James on how to work with a person's mental representation of time to change his experience of the present or trajectory into the future simply by altering his memory of the past, either adding to or deleting from it. It can produce magical results without using a spell! *Hmmph!*

There is a transcribed lecture by a famous psychiatrist from the Continent, Dr. Jung, on the nature of the shadow, with a stark circle in the mage's hand around a section:

How can I be substantial if I do not cast a shadow? I must have a dark side also if I am to be whole.

What's next? You open a book, *Utopias Within Reach.*

"Agh!!!" You cover your ears as the horrid thing crackles with electricity and briefly blasts out a cacophony of shouting voices that leave you singed and your ears ringing in pain.

The book quiets down, and as you recover, you find the book contains a worthless collection of predictable political speeches with a faux cover to disguise its nature as a trap. You should have known. Mage Greene wasn't one for rhetoric.

YOU LOSE 2D6 VITALITY POINTS.
CONTINUE TO SUCCESS.

WHEN YOU SUCCEED:

A lead at last! Fresh scone crumbs give it away. Inside a book on alternative magic is a scribbled note mentioning Mad Muse. The page shows an occult sigil and refers to another tome, *Grimoire of Lost Souls*, for casting details. Drawing the sigil helps summon some kind of spirit to possess a person or machine.

You scour the office. Unfortunately, if Mage Greene had that book, he has taken with him!

Oh, wait... another huge clue! A bookmark in the mage's spellbook opens to a spell, *Viam Invenire*, which means something like "Point the Way". It is a powerful spell requiring premium spell dust, which you don't have, nor have ever even snorted! But, but... the spell can tell you the distance and direction to any object you draw. If the mage has the occult tome or a sigil on him, you can find him or at least more information.

"*Excellentissime!*" you can't help but cry out. But can you find premium dust to even cast this spell?

Finally, you find a letter. It's dated two days ago. It is a complaint. It briefly describes Slacks—your fellow Special Lieutenant Edward Slacks—as harassing a new recruit and being complicit in a romantic affair. The other airman's name is Henry Jones. Regulations strictly prohibit fraternization on base, particularly of this kind, and harassment isn't welcome.

Slacks enters the office.

You quickly drop the letter away in a drawer.

"Any luck?" he asks.

Quickly, you decide to keep your mouth shut as Mage Greene would do and play dumb.

"Not much," you reply. "A ton of books and papers here. I still believe he was working toward summoning something."

Slacks notices the damaged bookcase that you slammed against earlier when trying to open the safe.

"You're doing a bang-up job," he comments.

You both laugh.

He sits down across from you, leans in, and gets serious.

"I developed the photos. Here you go," as states as he hands you a packet. "And I have an idea…" He piques your curiosity. "… I've been on real cases before, at my last assignment. But I'd need full control of the reigns to really help you."

His brazen confidence surprises you. You take a breath. "How about you share your idea…" And then you stop, realizing why he has taken this tack. He wants credit for his work and a promotion as much as you do. "Oh, I see."

"Yeah, and let's be frank…" he leans in and shows his teeth. "I like you, or I wouldn't waste time annoying you, but this project needs a *man* on the job."

Now you are annoyed. In fact, you are fuming and would lose your temper if you were one to show anger, which is entirely what Slacks is tempting.

"You insult me," you say firmly and stand up. "I too have evidence and ideas and am pursuing them, thank you for clarifying your role." You are determined to solve this case, earn a promotion, and not let Slacks get under your skin.

"Well then, I'm all ears for your plans," he says snidely.

Hmm, you ponder. To cast Point the Way, you need premium spell dust. Alas, the mage's safe had none, you have none, and ordering some through the Supply Depot would take days at least. But if you recall correctly, for whatever reason, Slacks recently bragged he has some.

GO TO THE NEXT SCENE.

Scene #12

Who's a Little Devil?

You decide to ask Slacks for his premium spell dust. In exchange, you'll burn that complaint, which lies in a nearby drawer.

"Slacks?" you ask quietly, getting his attention.

"C?," he replies, looking up from the photos.

"I found this letter about you and Airman Henry Jones."

Slacks stops. "Ugh…"

"I suppose there's some discretion in how to handle it," you explain. You smile weakly. You are uncomfortable doing this. But it is also slightly thrilling.

He hangs his head, downcast.

"Yeah, I've got an issue," he says in a down voice.

**How do you convince Slacks?
Do you 1) act confident, 2) appeal to your
comradery, 3), emphasize reporting his
misconduct, or 4) stay casual?**

"You know we're pals," you start, getting closer and in a low tone. "I don't want to say anything. I mean, in the grand scheme of things, your sideways hobby isn't much really, and I'm hardly old fashioned. I can just burn the letter."

"Are you trying to blackmail me?" he asks.

"What? No," you reply. "It's a win for both of us."

He waits, his face neutral but his fingers nervous.

You continue. "I need some premium dust. Enough for…" Maybe you should ask for more than one? "…how about two vials?" You immediately regret phrasing it as a question. The Commander has told you on more than one occasion that you tend to be too polite.

"That's a bit," Slacks replies. "I don't have that. I'd have to snag some on the sly. That could get me into more trouble…."

You back-peddle, immediately feeling dirty. "One vial is fine. You were just telling me last week you had one."

"Yeah," he replies without commitment.

Curious, you ask, "How did you get hold of premium anyway? Or should I not ask?"

"C, I've got ambitions too. And as I said, I've been on cases before. I'm smart enough to save a little for the future."

TRY AN ACT OF CHARM.
(X=D20 + 3 IF CHARM IS A GIFT.
ADD +3 IF YOU ACT CONFIDENT.)

OPTION: IF YOU WANT, YOU CAN CAST A CHARM SPELL. THIS REQUIRES YOU SPEND 1 VITALITY POINT NOW TO ADD +2 MORE TO YOUR D20 ROLL.

YOU FAIL IF X IS LESS THAN 17:

Slacks voice firms. "Decent plan, C. But honestly, I don't care if you report my affair. That bloke, Henry, and I are done anyway. And I need a change of pace from this rat's nest." He emphasizes the word "rat," perhaps referring to you.

You weren't expecting this response.

"Yeah," Slacks adds. "I really don't care." He smiles now, with no sign of nerves. Was his downcast demeanor just an act? Or is his confidence now an act? "But I get the sense you need something. You really need it, 'cos you're all proper and like to please big daddy." By "big daddy" he means the Commander. "And aren't you a pal who doesn't normally stoop to blackmail? Whatever possessed you, C? Let me spare you that."

Slacks, so cool and brazen, surprises you.

Slacks adds: "I might help you though, as a favor...."

You start thinking through options. But mostly, this all feels wrong. This is a reminder to stay on the straight and narrow in the future. Why did you even consider blackmail? It's not like you. It's certainly not what Mage Greene would have done or even contemplated. Yes, as Slacks just said, what possessed you?

Slacks starts to walk away and says a step above a whisper, "How about you get some on the sly yourself."

"No!" you say. "I mean, let's talk about it."

He comes back and whispers in your ear. "How about you tell me the time, Airman." By "time" he means romance.

Ugh, you think. "What? No," you say. "No way."

"Fair enough." He smiles.

You two now stand face to face, like in one of those gunslinger films. In theory, you are colleagues who work together. In practice, you are a local favorite here and he's angling to earn a promotion over you.

"I know you ain't Richy Rich," Slacks says. "How are you going to compensate me?"

You're unsure. You haven't been in this situation or seen this side of him before. Didn't only villains in comic books behave like this? You reply, "Maybe something else? I didn't mean to bring this up that way. I'm sorry."

"Just give me that report, and maybe a little favor down the line, as pals," he says. "And I respect you saying 'no'. You have standards, even when desperate."

"The report is ashes. And I owe you," you agree. "Let's do that." It's unexpected but not so terrible. At least it's not blackmail.

Slacks spits into his hand and extends it for a shake like honor between gentle bandits. "You owe me."

A small but sharp surge of revulsion shakes you, but what choice do you have? He has just outplayed you. And again, what possessed you to try this?

You grasp his hand and shake on it.

"I'll leave the packet of dust in your suggestion box, mate," he says matter of factly. "And you keep your word."

When returning from Command School and taking up your post here, you put out a "suggestion box". It's a modern idea to hear from the enlisted rather than ignore them. "They'll feel involved!" you were told. Since setting it up, no one is using it except to offer lewd jokes.

"I keep my word," you reply. You sigh.

YOU OWE SLACKS. THIS MAY COST YOU LATER.
CONTINUE TO SUCCESS.

WHEN YOU SUCCEED:

Slacks agrees with a wink of complicity.

"Glad we worked this out," you say to smooth things.

"Of course. Good thing I've taken a shine to you. And I'll start analyzing those samples from the Redkite." As he exits, he adds, "Oh... what spell are you trying to cast? I ask in case something goes sideways and you need help." He smiles.

"It'll be fine," you say vaguely as Mage Greene would have.

Slacks leaves, and while you wait for him to get that spell dust, you neatly write out what you have discovered so far, compiling your notes into a dossier.

OPTION: IF YOU WISH, YOU CAN SPEND 1 VITALITY
TO MAKE A PERFECT COPY OF THE OCCULT SIGIL BY
CASTING A REPLICATE SPELL. DECIDE 'YES' OR 'NO'.

You open Mage Greene's spellbook and review the "Point the Way" spell. You've never cast it, but you watched the mage cast it once when you were eleven after you lost a favorite toy. Fortunately, besides magic, one of your gifts is your memory for details.

YOU LOSE 1 SANITY POINT, OR 3 SANITY POINTS
IF YOU COPIED THE OCCULT SIGIL IN DETAIL.
GO TO THE NEXT SCENE.

13 March 1936

Dear Comdr. Hollingsworth,

The attached dossier regards the mysterious disappearance of all persons aboard spellship Redkite after it departed our base this day. The investigation is ongoing. Herein is a summary of potentially relevant information.

Redkite departed this morning as scheduled with a spellpilot, twelve airmen, and Major Mage Greene. Redkite radioed in earlier than expected at a key way-point and returned soon after with no crew. All cargo was present including an ergo, a technocrat (aka 'Mad Muse'), and a strongbox with unknown but cleared civilian contents.

Reconnaissance of the spellship revealed unnatural dust, fleeting life signs in an ergo and technocrat, bloodstains, and ergo prints to and from the spellhelm. The ergo was briefly aggressive to investigators, animated by an unseen force. No serious injuries sustained. The ship's log shows two unusual five-minute gaps as if it did not record (or time did not pass).

A search for clues has revealed a sigil (magical geometry). Mage Greene book-marked a spell that summons a dark "spirit" specific to this sigil. Efforts are underway to learn more about it. It is possible Mage Greene cast the spell to improve the technocrat, only to lose control of the spirit.

Lt. Mancy is leading a squad along the ship's flight path looking for clues and perhaps to locate missing persons, while Sp.Lt. Slacks is confirming that dust from the ship is not organic remains.

Additional updates will be forthcoming.

Sp.Lt. C. Ernest   *C. Ernest*

Scene #13

Point the Way

You return to your quarters.

It's 1330 hours.

It's past lunchtime. You consider grabbing an apple and some jerky to appease your grumbling stomach. But you recall that Mage Greene fasted before challenging spells. "Best to vomit only lightly," he once advised with whimsy.

Briefly, you consider aborting this uncertain path. As best you can tell, the mage—an otherwise wise and gentlemanly soul, well-acquainted with magic—got in over his head with a dark spell. What would possess *him* to do that? Or was the spellship's end due to bad luck, a curse by an unknown shadowy foe, or... moral weakness on his part? The last of those is hard to imagine.

You shiver.

Mage Greene would go out on a limb for you if circumstances were reversed, and he would urge you to solve the mystery. Even if your spell leads to random turns or dead-ends, what would you do without the kind man who's been your father, not to mention the others, all of whom as good mates, who are missing?

Come on, Lieutenant, you chastise yourself, *promote your arse!* You feel you must act.

In the loo, at the sink, you snort the premium orange dust that Slacks gave you. You hold up the scrap of paper with the sigil and cast "Point the Way". You have no idea if it will work or how casting it will affect you.

How do you improve your chances?
Do you 1) utter a prayer, 2) recall Mage Greene casting it years ago, 3) imagine yourself impressing the Commander, 4) think of your slain parents?

As you weave your fingers and hands in an elaborate pattern, you utter an incantation: "Hidge pidge, reveal the nidge where this sigil lies with the most tidge." To an untrained eye and ear, the whole thing is like a child acting out a nonsense poem. But to a wizard with a playful side like Mage Greene, no spell is too simple or complex to escape a moment of humor.

TRY AN ACT OF INTELLECT.
(X=D20 + 3 IF INTELLECT IS A GIFT. ADD +3 IF YOU RECALL MAGE GREENE CASTING IT. ADD +5 MORE IF YOU MAGICALLY MADE A PERFECT COPY OF THE SIGIL IN SCENE #12.)

YOU FAIL IF X IS LESS THAN 15:

The mirror glows and ripples briefly but fails to show anything before the magic dies out like a match stick that fails to catch flame.

Alas, you did not cast the spell correctly. Plainly, this spell is about more than speaking an incantation and making some intricate hand motions. You were not prepared to channel such a large charge of energy.

YOU MUST ROLL AGAIN, AND IF YOU FAIL, YOU MUST KEEP TRYING UNTIL YOU SUCCEED.
EACH TRY COSTS 2 VITALITY AND 1 SANITY POINT. REMEMBER, IF NEEDED, YOU CAN USE THE HEALING WAND YOU FOUND EARLIER.

WHEN YOU SUCCEED:

The tiny loo's mirror lights up and ripples like a fount.
In it, you see an old man in town with a book. You make out part of the book's title, ...*the Atlan Empire*... As for the old

man's house—*where is it?* you mumble—it sits at the intersection of Hardie and Lakesicht Avenues just a couple miles from here. You have seen this old man before! He is a retired teacher and old colleague of Mage Greene's. You thought he passed away some years ago. Apparently not.

Now you know where to go next.

CASTING THE SPELL COSTS YOU 5 VITALITY.
IF THIS KNOCKS YOU TO 0 VITALITY OR LESS, YOU
DON'T DIE. INSTEAD, YOU SOON BRIEFLY AWAKEN,
CAN USE A POTION TO HEAL, AND SUFFER A -3
PENALTY ON THE NEXT SCENE'S CHECK.

GO TO THE NEXT SCENE.

PART IV

OFF BASE,
ON COURSE

Scene #14

Jaunt into Town

You head off base and into town.

Given the morning's dank weather and distance, a cab is sensible. But the day is finally warming up with the sun peeking out in spots, and a brisk walk—with umbrella—will let you think with minimal distractions. Besides, cab drivers are known as "curious cabbies" and "red ears" for a reason.

You take in the town on your walk. It relies mostly on textiles, mining, and fishing. There is also a mammoth electro-tech plant that caters to the airbase, and you spot more electric busses and *zizzies* (electric scooters) than on your last jaunt.

The town buzzes with all manner of folks. Roaming bands of kids are riding bicycles. As a kid, you often biked, but the last time you took out a bicycle, the guys had a good laugh on your account. Workers done with their morning shift are heading home from the town's mine. As High Street shops appear, you spot fashionable women—short skirts just noticeable under their coats—with fancy heels and bobbed cuts. If magazines are a clue, bob cuts are now out of style, but maybe small towns are last to hear and adopt the ways of the big cities?

You consider avoiding Parade Street. Its bars, tattoo shops, and massage parlors cater to airmen such as you. Well, not like you, like the enlisted. The street tends to be rowdy, bawdy, and a touch dangerous, even during the day.

"Hey Airman, it's warm inside," a local cat-calls you from an open red door to a seedy-looking corner building.

A magic shop catches your eye. It's halfway down Parade Street. In bold, brassy letters it reads, "Madame Mikka's Magic." It's swanky by the looks of it, catering to gifted folks like you. You wonder why it's here and not on High Street.

The Crown regulates all magic use, of course. *Gee*, you realize, *here's a spot to buy premium dust!* This didn't even occur to you earlier! *But for the best*, you muse. It would've cost dearly, and you'd have to show your official magician's card, which is only authorized for basic dust. *Hmph.* Sometimes rules are annoying.

"Oy!" several ruffians bump into you.

"I know you, yes I do," the skinny one says. "You're Virgi." That's an epithet for an innocent but uptight person.

The brawnier one pinches you and wraps his beefy arm around your neck. "How about you use your magic, ginger, to light my ciggi," he growls.

"There's no need for trouble," you say, perhaps too late.

TRY AN ACT OF BRAWN.
(X=D20 + 3 IF BRAWN IS A GIFT.)

YOU FAIL IF X IS LESS THAN 15:

The ruffians harrass you mercilessly. They're baiting you into casting a spell, but anything flashy can get you into trouble.

YOU LOSE 1D6 VITALITY POINTS FIGHTING THEM OFF.
YOU MUST KEEP TRYING UNTIL YOU SUCCEED.

WHEN YOU SUCCEED:

You don't see constables about.

"*Summone avem!*," you whisper, calling for feathered help.

A beautiful raven flies down, startling the ruffians as it caws and pecks wildly at them. *Cawcaw! Cawcaw!*

"Agh!" they yell as they cover their faces and run off.

"Ha ha ha!" From across the street, several old men at chess and cards laugh at the scene.

YOU LOSE 1 VITALITY POINT POWERING THE SPELL.
GO TO THE NEXT SCENE.

SCENE #15

STRANGE OLD MAN

You walk to Hardie and Lakesicht Avenues. The area is stacked with older, stately residences. At the corner stands the house exactly as you saw in the mirror with your spell.

Job well done, you say to yourself, as Mage Greene would. The book you're looking for is somewhere in this house.

You wonder how best to approach the situation. Should you come as friendly but authoritative? And if so, what to say? Keep the truth to yourself or tell it as it is or a bit of both? Maybe being too mysterious will be rude, especially as a guest seeking a favor? What if you will need to study from the man's books for a while? Likely, he has the book you're looking for.

IF YOU HAVE LESS THAN MAXIMUM SANITY POINTS, THEN READ THE SECTION BELOW. OTHERWISE, GO NOW TO THE NEXT PAGE.

Another question pops into your mind. *Should I leave the book with him, borrow it, or steal it?*

Wait, what? You stop yourself.

You feel terribly odd. You feel dirty, even tainted. Why did you just think of stealing? Isn't this the second time today, or maybe the third?

Gosh! You admonish yourself. Certainly, you're no thief, are you? Not really. Everyone knows you are too by-the-book for that. Of course, there are plenty of things you might covet. When you were a kid, you liked candies, toy ray guns, and a painting of the moon called "Void Magic". But actually stealing? *No, that's not me, not now*, you reassure yourself.

You hammer the door's gothic knocker.

Nothing.

You ring the doorbell.

"Oh bother, I know, I'm coming!" a man's gravelly voice shouts from within.

After a bit, an old man opens the door. He has a kindly face. He's frumpy, unshaven, and still in his bedclothes under a house jacket. Thankfully, he doesn't smell ripe. For sure he's your old tutor, who was a very pleasant fellow.

"Come in, love," he exclaims, as if overjoyed.

"Hello," you say, "I hate to be a bother. You may recall..."

"What, of course. Come in, come in," he says cheerfully. "Make yourself comfortable. I've cleared the sofa for you."

His place is untidy, but the sofa is clear and clean. Books, notebooks, and strange electrotech abide on nearly every surface and lurk in every corner. You wonder if the electrotech devices are techno-magical instruments of some kind.

A tea kettle whistles from the kitchen.

"Ah, tea's ready. Do you still take milk?" He looks you over. "You're still skinny. Of course, you need some warm milk."

"How did you...," you start.

"The stars and a little mouse let me know company was coming," he says as if explaining.

You go to sit on the sofa as he gets tea.

A mouse darts across your path.

The old man comes in with two cups of tea.

"Don't mind Thomas," he says. He adds, "Fine uniform you've earned. Oh, I should offer to take your coat."

"I'm fine, really," you say. "I'm already out of it."

HOW DO YOU GET ANSWERS?
DO YOU 1) PATIENTLY HUMOR HIM, 2) REMINISCE
ABOUT OLD TIMES, 3) THINK OF WHAT MAGE
GREENE WOULD SAY OR DO, OR 4) GET SERIOUS
ABOUT THE POINT OF YOUR VISIT.

"You didn't just drop in to reminisce, yeah?" he asks lucidly. You wonder, is he merely acting addled? A bulge in his house jacket has the distinctive outline of a pistol.

"There're demons about in the dead of night, ya know?"

"Really? What do you mean?" you ask.

"Why do you think they got us under curfew?"

In a sense, the town has a curfew. It runs from midnight to sun-up, except on Friday nights, at the behest of the town's small but necessary pub scene. But it's common sense and not a response to an actual threat, at least as far as you know.

"Yes," you say. "That may be. And you're a close friend of Mage Greene? The wizard at the airbase. He's gone missing."

"Oh dear," he says, "his stars are for the hangman this week. He's been tempting fate lately, I should say," he confides.

"Did Mage Greene stop by recently?" you ask.

"I believe so, if my memory isn't fooling me." He looks over at a ledger or diary of some kind. "Yes, surely recently."

"Did he come for a book?" You hope he remembers it.

"Certainly," he replies as he gets up and rummages through a nearby stack of books that lack dust.

"Here she is!" He returns with a dusky book. It announces itself as *Grimoire of Lost Souls* by Drs. d'Luminar and L'Strange. A gold-gilded occult eye adorns its jet-black leather cover.

It's not the book you saw earlier in the mirror.

"Oh bother, this isn't it," he says, tossing it to the side. He gets up and grabs another, smaller, fancier book. It's *Occult Mysteries of the Atlan Empire* by Dr. Joan Carver. A photo on the jacket's back portrays a prim woman with an air of mystery.

"Joan here," he explains, tapping the cover, "is a wunder-kind. Lovely too. I met her once. Back then, she was wasting her time as junior faculty at Miskatonic University."

"Wasting time?" you ask.

"Oh, she's got the gift," he explains. "Like you, Airman Ernest, you've got the gift."

"Thank you," you reply.

"Though you have a few things to work out first," he says

seriously. "And please don't thank me for your magic."

You hope he hasn't turned sour. Old people can be like that. You try to move along. "I have a sketch..." you start to say.

TRY AN ACT OF CHARM.
(X=D20 + 3 IF CHARM IS A GIFT.
ADD +2 IF YOU PATIENTLY HUMOR HIM.)

YOU FAIL IF X IS LESS THAN 14:

The two of you sit and page through the book. He flips pages here and there, mumbling unfamiliar terms, with a glint of youthful excitement. Clearly, it's a costly book. It sports color photographic plates of ruins, including underwater ones.

"Here is one of my favorite vestiges, of the knight constellation..." he announces, pointing to a photograph of a relief of a strange octopus-like creature.

His rambling sounds a bit above your head: "... and at the end of time, an army of aberrant bio-constructs, an enigmatic race called ergons, were banished to a few minutes before the end of time, or so the colorful legend purports."

"What are vestiges?" you ask, backing up.

"Not much of anything, just tatters, really. Now here..."

You discretely cast an *Aiming* spell on him. Normally, you use it on yourself during target practice, but sometimes it helps someone get to the point, patient as you try to be.

"Oh dear," he admonishes, "you don't need that. Let me reminisce, will you, and let me impress upon you what you don't know, yet."

"Please accept my apology," you say, mortified. Normally, people don't notice. "I didn't mean to be rude. It's just, you know, we haven't seen each other in quite a while."

"Oh no?" he says, confused. "I saw you just last night."

You're not sure what he means.

"You'll understand sooner than you know," he adds in a kindly voice. He winks.

YOU LOSE 1 VITALITY POWERING YOUR AIMING SPELL.

WHEN YOU SUCCEED:

You show him the sketch you made of the sigil you found earlier. In Dr. Joan Carver's book, you two find that sigil. It's of a "lost spirit". The spirit's name is "Doomed Salu'im" and its title is "The Army at Time's Horizon".

"Very creative," you offer. Even in a world with actual monsters, people manage to still dream up worse ones.

"This kind of spirit" the old man explains, "is called a vestige, or it's called a vivilor if it appears in the flesh."

He goes on to explain that the spirit must be summoned using a ritual. Apparently, it's somewhat like a ghost. With help, it can briefly enjoy living life again through the eyes and ears of the person who conjures it. "In exchange," he adds with emphasis, "it provides that man, or woman, with power."

"The quest for power eventually comes at a price, doesn't it?" you offer, feeling at last that you have something to add.

"I'd say change comes at a price," he offers. "From my long years, I say." His eyes sparkle with knowing warmth.

That actually sounds much smarter, you think, though a bit pessimistic. Yes, in your short years, you have learned that life is shades of gray, and if it looks like a rainbow, it's probably best to run. Even your rescue and life in Avalon was merely light gray, the life of a soldier, not the musician you once dreamed of becoming as a boy, before the Great War.

"Thank you much," you say, "for your kind instruction."

IF YOU SAY GOODBYE NOW, GO TO SCENE #17 (PAGE 66). OTHERWISE, GO TO THE NEXT SCENE.

Doomed Salu'im
Army at Time's Horizon

Preparations: Firstly, draw Doomed Salu'im's seal with a masterwork hourglass nearby. The spirit, actually an army of splintered minds, responds well if you are a robot or have one with you. Alternatively, bring a vial of sand untouched by the passage of a millennia or more. Finally, cut eight tiny circles of flesh out of your body and eat the pieces. From each and all of the eight carved rings, eyes fly out and study you with close paranoia as you negotiate with the spirit.

Legend: The Salu'im are (or were? or will be?) "ergons," a fearsome and enigmatic race of interstellar beings—half-flesh, half-machine—that occult sages say came about from a hellish marriage of flesh-warping technology and pactmaking. Little is known about ergons because they care little for other sentient creatures, especially puny lesser beings like humans. Texts say they look like giant metallic squid that roam the vast voids of outer space. They are certainly driven to procreate, which for them means snatching soil, water, magic, creatures, atmosphere, and anything else they need in order to craft worlds where they can grow and harvest the parts needed to create more of their kind. Ergons divide themselves into bickering factions, but all speak of a massive unification event known as The Horizon, when their overlord, Salu Zed, emerges at the end of time to claim the whole universe. Fortunately for good and free creatures everywhere, this horrid plan malfunctions.

Powers: Doomed Salu'im toughens your body and mind to be like metal. The spirit also links you to the ergon collective to suddenly know a techno-magical power as easily as one checks out a library book. Your knowledge of history, mechanics, and war grows keen. Finally, by its power, you can move or bounce ahead in time.

SCENE #16

TOUCH OF DARKNESS

"See here kiddo," the old man continues, "before you run off to your destiny, know what the spirit grants by its pact. It makes you more like a machine, and get this, you can literally jump forward through time! Don't think I'm kidding."

"Not at all," you say, doing your best to be polite. Of course minor magic is real, and everyone knows from history books and the Seven Wonders of the World that a few truly powerful spells exist. But who could actually wield such power now, much less after a two-minute ritual?

"Can a spirit be summoned to possess a device rather than a person?" you ask him.

"Sneaky bastard!" he exclaims. At first, you wonder if he means you and feel insulted, but he means Mage Greene. "Uh, yes, one could bind a vestige into a machine."

"Did Mage Greene say anything about Mad Muse?"

"No, but perfecting her has been his passion for years. I'm unsurprised now that you mention it."

You're curious why the old man lives here in this little town. At least Mage Greene had access to military resources.

"You know," he says, grabbing your jacket, "you've got to listen to this part." He starts paging through the book until he gets to a passage about something called taint.

"What's taint?" you ask. You know it is associated with dark magic, like necromancy, but you want to hear his answer.

He reads aloud: "Everything touched, heard, or seen of a spirit or its sigil leaves a residue. Most often, residue appears as profuse dust or grime."

"That explains the layer of dust in the spellship!" you say.

"A spellship's involved? Why didn't you say so!"

"Well yes, though that's classified. Sorry."

"Very well." He continues reading: "In a person, residue

wells up as nausea or intrusive thoughts of vices, such as lust or envy, which grows more acute with added exposure as the taint accumulates. The result may be a crime aligned with the dark recesses of the person's hidden nature, a kind of mirror or shadow."

"We don't want that, do we!" Even as you speak, you are reminded of your dream and odd behavior today.

Which reminds you... "Might I borrow this book?" you ask. "Just for a day or two. I promise to return it."

He looks aghast. "I shan't part with it." He grabs it and holds it tightly to his chest. "It's too dangerous." He looks at your drawing of the sigil. "Did you draw that?" he asks.

"I copied it," you explain.

"Geometry itself has great power. It is tainted."

"Oh?" You are incredulous. "Merely by drawing..." You feel an urge to trace the sigil's delicate lines with your finger.

TRY AN ACT OF FAITH.
(X=D20 + 3 IF FAITH IS A GIFT.)
IF X IS LESS THAN 9, YOU LOSE 1D6 SANITY POINTS.
OTHERWISE, YOU LOSE 1 SANITY POINT.

All of a sudden, you are at the door as he's showing you out. "... and the end result, my young student, is insanity."

"Sounds awful," you reply.

"No worries, there are worse things in life, let me tell you. My wife could too, may the Creator rest her soul in peace." He chuckles. "You're a brave one, I'll give you that."

Before you leave, you jot down the book's name and Dr. Joan Carver's information. You make a mental note to send off a message of inquiry to her office to order the book.

You wave goodbye as you carefully close the garden gate.

YOU GAIN ONE BOON THAT YOU CAN USE TO GAIN
A +5 BONUS TO ANY 1 ROLL LATER IN THE GAME.
GO TO THE NEXT SCENE.

Scene #17
A Perilous Path

As you head home, night falls, rain patters, and you think it all through. It sounds like Mage Greene was dabbling in occult magic, conjuring spirits, or at least one spirit called "Doomed Salu'im". *Isn't its name enough to know not to mess with it?* You wonder. The old man said it could travel through time, which was straight out of a comic and impossibly fanciful. *Whatever.* The mage's experiment failed, the spirit got loose, maybe it possessed the ergo? And its residue coated the ship. But what happened to the hapless crew?

Bam! Someone clobbers you on the back of the head.

Try an Act of Brawn.
(X=D20 + 3 if Brawn is a gift.)

_____

You fail if X is less than 10:

You scuffle. There are two assailants. They are hooded, but you recognize them as the two ruffians from earlier on Parade Street. Now they have clubs and knives. You are awfully dizzy from the initial clobbering. They do their best to kill you.

You lose 1D6 vitality points.
You must keep trying until you succeed.

_____

When you succeed:

You scramble away and race with fear back to the airbase.

Go to the next scene.

PART V

NIGHT IS
A NEW DAY

SCENE #18

GOOD OL' DAYS

Back from town, you head to the mess hall. You're starving! Mealtime is almost over and many airmen are out under Mancy's leadership in the mountains in search of the lost crew. No doubt they are now enjoying rations in the cold drizzle under a nearly moonless sky. As you sit alone and quietly gobble down dinner, you reflect.

Three years ago, as an enlisted airman, you sat in this same spot when you broke the most amazing news of your life to your mates. That day, the Commander had recognized your potential and nominated you for Command School!

Wow! Command School!

Though you and your mates had grown close, you had to say yes. Like true friends, they surely wanted the best for you.

Then a year ago, you returned to base as a newly commissioned officer. On the night following you return, your old pals—none officers—threw a cracking party for you. Quickly, you were all rip-roaring, smashing drunk. That takes you back.

REMINISCE

"Hey," an airman named Reggie calls you to, "now that you got a flashy new ribbon, you gonna show us some real magic?"

"Oy mate," another snaps back to him, "he's Special Lieutenant to you. Show respect."

You burp for their amusement. After Command School, you rank above them but you don't let that go to your head.

Everyone has a good laugh.

"Gentlemen," you reassure them, "I don't see, hear, nor smell anything in the least suspicious tonight, or in this hall ever, if you know what I mean."

"Oh yeah?" one asks as a challenge.

"Now," you add, "I will show off..."

One of your best mates grabs Reggie and holds his hand, palm flat and fingers spread, down on the table.

"Time for a handjob, Reggie," one of them taunts.

You grab up a steak knife.

"*Actum perfectum*," you incant and kiss the knife.

"What are you... You're mad!" Reggie exclaims.

"Spread 'em wide," another airman says, referring to his fingers, "You don't want to lose any of your small bits."

"Agh!" Reggie shouts, drunk, excited, and terrified.

You start your knife show, rapidly stabbing the knife between his fingers, hoping to not actually strike him.

TRY AN ACT OF AGILITY.
(X=D20. ADD +3 IF AGILITY IS A GIFT.)

IF X IS 15 OR MORE, YOU GAIN A BOON. YOU CAN ADD +5 TO ANY ACT OF AGILITY LATER IN THE GAME.

The airmen swear with glee and cheer you.

Show over, Reggie pulls away his hand, nursing it closely to his chest. "Frickin' monsters you all are," he yells, shaking. "One of you loathsome gents get me another drink before I puke."

You settle them down. "Here's a toast to all of us. May war stay far away and friends remain close!"

"Cheers!" they toast.

"And know I'm still Airman Ernest at heart." Sarcastically, you add, "I will be confiscating your records, girly magazines, and comics all for my own amusement."

"Hear, hear!" several shout mindlessly. Others groan.

"And... you can trust when things don't go well for you, I'll use a butter knife as often as I can."

Most of them laugh. One, in particular, does not. For a moment, he betrays a grim look as the festivities continue.

A month later, that grim-faced airman took advantage of your friendship after abusing some mind-bending medications he stole from the infirmary. Those benzos affected his performance. There was an explosion but no one was hurt, fortunately. On that day, you admitted that life is different as an officer. You must suss out things. Digging into your friend's life— *or better said, that airman's life*—was painful and eye-opening.

GO TO THE NEXT SCENE.

SCENE #19

SHIFT OF PERSPECTIVE

You retire to your quarters. You pour a glass of wine from your stash, intending to dive into Mage Greene's notes and further research the sigil. But in today's unopened mail is the latest issue of one of your favorite comics, *Mind Spy. Hmm...*

IF YOU HAVE LESS THAN MAXIMUM SANITY POINTS, THEN READ THE SECTION BELOW. OTHERWISE, JUMP NOW TO THE NEXT SECTION.

––––––––––––––––

You tear open the comic's paper wrapper and dive in.

Most comics follow the lives of *Hierians*, people who suddenly blossom with supernatural powers and can fly, often in their adolescence. Of course, the comics usually aren't about the real hierians, who occasionally feature in the news but are otherwise top secret and fairly rare. Maybe a dozen defend the whole Commonweal, or so the news says.

Your comic here features Mind Spy, a fictional hierian who can see and hear through walls and even step through them on occasion. At the same time, he's also somewhat clumsy, which makes his adventures funny and relatable.

In the last issue, Mind Spy caught a glimpse of a beautiful woman in an enemy Gath castle that he was investigating. Would he ignore her? Or more likely, would he do something cheeky, which is what you figure makes *Mind Spy* so popular.

But... Mage Greene is missing, and you're up for a promotion if you can solve the biggest case of your young career. *Grow up, Special Lieuy,* you chide yourself. You close the comic.

YOU GAIN A "MIND SPY CLUE" YOU MAY USE LATER. CONTINUE BELOW.

Time for work. Mage Greene's notes are dense and you're tired. Maybe it's actually time for more magic? After all, one spell advanced the case a long way today.

You refresh your wine glass and pull out your academy primer on basic magic. Just a few pages in, you encounter a "Read Runes" spell.

Dang! You realize that spell would have instantly analyzed the sigil for you, with no need to get premium dust or trek into town. *Gee,* you imagine, what if you had mastered that spell instead of, say, a milk-toast "Light" spell and used a flashlight instead? In the early years, you were pretty timid with magic, and even now you tend to stick to easy spells. Well, you know why you learned "Light" first, given your childhood.

Even now, you can intensely recall the pungent smell of sulfur, like you are back in those last days of the Great War, before you were rescued, hiding in the attic, when devils came to town. Your parents were downstairs shouting and pleading for mercy. Never again would you be stuck in the dark.

Put away all that, Special Lieutenant you scold yourself. You drain your wine glass. How about some ice water? Mage Greene once told you that a glass of water after a glass of wine goes a long to avoid a hangover.

In the loo, you run the water cold and splash your face and... the mirror looks odd.

Yes, it's not just you. The mirror is tilted, but it shouldn't be because it's bolted on and has always been straight. Your memory is clear. Maybe the wine has skewed your perception?

The mirror ripples as it did earlier when you cast "Point the Way". You study it closely, following the ripples.

"What in the Nine Hells?" you mutter.

HOW DO YOU REACT?
DO YOU 1) AVERT YOUR GAZE FROM THE MIRROR,
2) SPLASH MORE COLD WATER BEFORE STUDYING IT,
OR 3) TOUCH IT?

You consider the possibilities. Is this a residual effect of the earlier spell? Is it due to the wine or maybe food poisoning? Or did Lt. Slacks give you impure dust or did he spike it? Your mind spins possible scenarios. What if the wanker poisoned you?

TRY AN ACT OF ENDURANCE.
(X=D20 + 3 IF ENDURANCE IS A GIFT.
APPLY -5 IF YOU TOUCHED THE MIRROR.)

YOU FAIL IF X IS LESS THAN 10:

You're woozy. A horrid wave of vertigo slams you. You barely steady yourself on the lip of the sink even as your knees buckle and stomach somersaults. You get down to the toilet...

Bluh! You retch repeatedly. *Bluh! Bluh!*

There goes two glasses of wine and most of your dinner. Slowly—feeling shaky—you wash up.

YOU LOSE 1 VITALITY POINT.
CONTINUE TO SUCCESS.

WHEN YOU SUCCEED:

The mirror ripples and shows you younger. You are opening a little spellbook in order to learn "Read Runes" rather than "Light". There you are, making a choice. What if you could revisit the past and choose differently?

For a moment, you feel as if you do in fact know "Read Runes." Startled, you quickly push the feeling away.

Chills run up your spine.

IF YOU EXIT THE LOO, GO TO SCENE #22 (PAGE 80). OR IF YOU STAY, KEEP READING.

Surely, you look slightly different in the mirror, maybe stronger or more comely? You peer in. You smile and frown. You splash your face again, rub your eyes, turn on and off the light, and observe the mirror closely.

Tiny ripples cross the glassy surface. You put out your finger, drawn to poke at it.

The mirror shows you just a few years ago in Command School. You're standing in a hallway watching a classmate from then, a smart-mouthed and cocky chap named Sarksman. He's holding the attention of another classmate, a fine gal named Maribel. You're there, trembling on the inside, scared of making a fool of yourself, of being rejected. You hardly dated in school.

"Wow!" you exclaim. You just stand there, stunned.

You wipe sweat off your brow with a trembling hand. What if you'd acted in that moment? Can you change the past?

WHO DO YOU PURSUE?
IF YOU PURSUE MARIBEL, TURN THE PAGE TO SCENE #20A. OR, IF YOU PURSUE SARKSMAN, JUMP TO SCENE #20B (PAGE 76).

GO IMMEDIATELY TO YOUR CHOSEN SCENE. YOU CANNOT STOP TO RECOVER.

Scene #20A

Flower in the Rain

In the mirror, you are back in time two years ago. You watch yourself get up the steel to steal Maribel, asking her out in front of your competition, Sarksman.

You gasp as she says, "yes!" She is delighted.

How do you make this "new" memory? Do you 1) focus on sensory details, 2) push the limits of your imagination, or 3) believe in yourself?

Head down, eyes closed, hands clenching the sink, you review your "new" memories with Maribel.

You two kiss for the first time.

Later, on your second date for tea, you two get soaked in a sudden downpour when you both forget umbrellas.

These new memories ripple through your storehouse of experiences, recoloring everything.

Now you are writing Maribel a letter soon after you two graduated and you returned to the airbase.

Try an Act of Faith. ($X = D20 + 3$ if Faith is a gift. Add $+2$ if you believe in yourself.)

You fail if X is less than 12:

You stagger back, dizzy, sweating, and shaking, almost violently. You grip the sink. As lovely as the vision is, the magic at play is overwhelming.

"You're hyperventilating, Ernest," you coach yourself.

"Take in big breaths and ease 'em out slowly." You fear to even take a peek up at the mirror. You hold your head in your hands to keep a hold of yourself as you crack up.

YOU LOSE 1D3 VITALITY AND LOSE 1 SANITY. KEEP REPEATING THIS SECTION UNTIL YOU SUCCEED.

WHEN YOU SUCCEED:

You focus. You and Maribel are kissing in wet cloths as you head to your dorm room. You unbutton her blouse...

This moment and more flood your mind. You recall her sweet perfume, soft skin, the calming touch of her hand on your chest that relaxes you. You are on your knees, bending back, with her on your thighs. You bring her closer to you, into your arms. You hear only her breathing, and she is incredibly warm.

Just minutes ago, these memories hadn't been yours, but they are now! Upon going to Command School, you were so determined to fall in love, but it didn't happen. But now it did!

The vision ends. The mirror calms and is still.

Patter, patter. Your stomach, heart, and mind race. Before making an utter fool of yourself, you leap up and—on a hunch—rifle through your drawer of knickknacks.

Wow! Therein lies a neatly folded letter from Maribel replying to your letter to her. A kiss seals it and a dried rose petal adorns it. Yes, there is proof! You changed the past!

Wait, what? You can't believe this. *This is impossible.*

Does this mean a change of events affected Maribel too? As in, presently does she too have different memories? Did you just change some young woman's life from some other timeline? And if so, why do you still remember what happened "instead"? Or more likely, are you completely delusional?

BOOST ALL "ACTS OF CHARM" BY +2 FROM NOW ON. GO TO SCENE #21 (PAGE 78).

Scene #20b
Fire in the Grotto

In the mirror, you are back in time two years ago. You watch yourself get up the courage to ask Sarksman for a "stroll in the park" in front of your competition, Maribel.

"There's this lovely grotto," he suggests. "Some say the statues whisper their secrets to those they like. How about it?"

How do you make this "new" memory?
Do you 1) focus on sensory details,
2) push the limits of your imagination,
or 3) believe in yourself?

"Do you believe in true love?" you ask as you two walk. Mage Greene once brought up this question at a fancy dinner party when you were a kid, and you spent the week afterward asking everyone you met, fascinated to hear their answers.

"How does it go..." Sarksman replies, "Whenever I climb, I am followed by a dog called 'Ego.'" By this, he refers to self love. He is quoting that stormy Gath philosopher, Nietzsche.

"Cheeky," you reply. He makes you work for his soft side.

"Or, you mean..." He quotes, "It is not a lack of love, but a lack of friendship that makes unhappy marriages."

"You play with me," you offer gently, stopping. You take in his chiseled features with foppish hair and handsome suit.

"We play along with life, or not," he replies. He bites his lip. You lock onto each other's eyes.

Try an Act of Faith.
(X=D20 + 3 if faith is a gift.
Add +2 if you believe in yourself.)

_____

You fail if X is less than 12:

The night takes on a chill, the park darkens, and mirror fogs as if the scene runs away from you. The loo smells of sulfur.

Hmm. You consider, maybe not every path in life is possible to walk down. Some paths—most—are blocked? Instead of a little shift in events, you might cause mayhem. Or maybe not. You're curious and choose to push forward, wiping the fogged mirror to discover how far you can go.

CONTINUE TO SUCCESS.

WHEN YOU SUCCEED:

You focus. You and Sarksman are kissing in the grotto's soft brush. You unbutton his shirt and trousers....

This moment and more flood your mind. He takes you in his arms. You warm each other against the chill. Your whole body fills with warmth like an oven as he takes to you. His grip is... unyielding like stone, and... rough like coal...

You pull back, surprised and... *Agh!* Sarksman sports stubby horns, ruddy pebble skin, and a forked leathery tail.

What?! You scuttle back, terrified. From a quick look, he isn't a devil but maybe his grandpa was? He looks mortified too.

The vision ends in cries, tears, and flames.

The mirror calms and is still.

Just minutes ago, these memories hadn't been yours, but they are now. You reason, his devilish blood wasn't his fault, and it was likely the source of his magic, but you've had enough devils for a lifetime! Your heart and mind race with fear.

You scan your room in search of answers to this terrifying magic. Above your bed hangs the holy cross of St. Cuthbert.

Wait! That cross wasn't there before! When did you get religion? Apparently, you got some on that night two years ago.

BOOST ALL "ACTS OF FAITH" BY +2 FROM NOW ON.
YOU LOSE 1D3 VITALITY AND 1 SANITY.
GO TO THE NEXT SCENE.

Scene #21

Backlash

You lie down, disoriented and amazed. You feel it: *This is magic!* Real, powerful, amazing magic like in the comics!

But did you do this? And how? You just relived a memory of a relationship that supposedly never was.

"Holy frick!" you whisper.

Perhaps you are delusional. *Yes*, you reason, *that's it*. You are going crazy. But even now, the weight of the other, original timeline is slipping away as the new one washes over.

What did the old man say? Every interaction with the occult, either the Atlan book—what was its title?—or Mad Muse, the sigil, or whatever, taints a mortal in body and mind.

"Yes, I need help", you mumble in what feels like a brief lucid moment. Just today, you've suffered flashbacks and urges to steal, and you tried to blackmail a fellow officer. Even a wanker like Slacks, who curses, ridicules, and bullies, who has likely gotten the slip on you, that bloody maggot...

"Calm down, Airman Ernest," you say to calm yourself, "you don't talk or think that way or have these feelings."

You feel dizzy and burning hot.

Oh no! You recognize this feeling. When someone channels magic without spell dust, the price is a backlash.

Try an Act of Endurance.
(X=D20 + 3 if Endurance is a gift.)

If x is less than 15, then you fail, losing 2d6 vitality points and 1d3 sanity points. Or, if pass, you lose 1d6 vitality and 1 sanity point. If you survive, you sleep and heal 15 vitality points from rest. Go to the next scene.

Part VI

Bodies & Souls
Lost & Found

SCENE #22

COST OF SERVICE

You jog out to Hanger Two. It's just after dawn, 0600 hours, and cold enough to see your breath. Minutes ago, an airman came to your room and woke you with news. Thankfully, you fell asleep last night in uniform and were mostly ready to go. Whatever happened last night feels like a foggy dream.

As the smallest hanger, Two is for prop planes and cargo. Lieutenant Mancy and the Commander are talking just inside the door while the Sergeant is off looking over a dozen corpses laid out neatly on the hanger's cold cement.

"Bad news, C," Mancy says heavily. "We found bodies. They were down a ridge near Paladin's Peak."

You scan the corpses. They are gray, battered, and wet. Most of their faces are frozen with a look of surprise and horror. One is peaceful. Likely he was sleeping? As a gesture of kindness, at least someone had gone around and closed their eyes. You don't spot Mage Greene among them.

Mancy continues. "Circling birds gave away their site."

"Excellent work," the Commander says to her, sincere and downcast. He knows these men, at least by appearance from the daily routine, as do you and Mancy. The Sergeant, tending to them, knows them best. "Cause of death?" the Commander asks.

"Best we can tell, violent impact with the ground," Mancy says, "as if falling from a great height."

"But Mage Greene survived?" the Commander asks.

"Miraculously," she affirms.

You rejoice inside with the great news about your mentor, even if the rest onboard perished.

"I suspect he got off a *Feather Fall* spell," you explain. "It would cause him to fall slowly... like a feather. Is he in the..."

"Yes, but..." Mancy says, cutting off your elevating mood.

"But what?" you ask.

"I should warn you. We found him naked and crazy, terrified of his own clothing and babbling in some alien tongue."

You wonder, *what could push him past the brink of sanity?*

Ugh!" The fallen airman nearest you stirs, moaning in slow agony. He is trying to get up despite his wounds.

So he lives? Instinctively, you move to help him. He's your pal, Reggie. But his eyes are pitch-black and skin is taut gray with many holes. His wounds do not bleed. He emits no breath in the morning's cold. *Hmm, that's odd*, you wonder.

"Agh!!!" he gurgles. He attacks you!

TRY AN ACT OF BRAWN.
(X=D20 + 3 IF BRAWN IS A GIFT.)

YOU FAIL IF X IS LESS THAN 9:

You tussle with zombie Reggie. He grapples you and tries to bite you, but misses, as tiny brackish tentacles wriggle from the many holes that pockmark his body. *Eeee!*

YOU LOSE 1 VITALITY AND 1 SANITY POINT.
YOU MUST TRY AGAIN AND REPEAT THIS SECTION
UNTIL YOU SUCCEED.

WHEN YOU SUCCEED:

Mancy strides over cooly, and when she gets a clean shot, she blasts zombie Reggie in the side of the head. "Just in case," she says as he falls inanimate.

"Thanks," you say. Shaken, you move back and scan over the other bodies. All the rest are still but who knows.

"Best if we head-shot the rest," the Commander offers.

GO TO THE NEXT SCENE.

Scene #23

What You See
is Not What You Get

Next, you all head over to the infirmary to check on and hopefully interview Mage Greene, addled though he might be. You are excited to see him. What amazing news that he lives!

While walking over, you wonder, *what exactly occurred to you last night?* Was it a dream? Did you actually use the loo mirror to change your past? Did you actually make love back in school? It feels real. There's evidence, yes? Or was it just a weird nightmare after getting riled up by a comic book? You feel ridiculous.

You enter the infirmary.

Doc "Rabbit" is there. He is the base's medical officer. He keeps a hutch of rabbits. Some say he runs experiments on them. Others say he talks with them. You don't know him well. Though older, he recently transfered to the base.

Doc Rabbit is examining the mage and taking samples. The mage is laid out flat and semi-conscious on a steel exam table, perhaps because regular beds can't hold his goliath frame.

You edge closer to take a look while holding back a lump in your throat and dis-ease in your stomach.

Poor Mage Greene: his skin, normally bright green, is now deep ashen gray, and tiny rivulets of olive-colored goo, akin to lamp oil, trickle from his orifices.

"... doll bricks," the mage mumbles. His eyes dart wildly as he spouts gibberish. "Goldilocks had hair down to her favorite flower, and by the stove snaked ten gold coins, each a fast color..."

Mancy and the sergeant give you pained looks.

"Maybe he's trying to communicate," you offer hopefully.

"Your diagnosis, Doc?" the Commander asks.

"Ooooh, severe aphasia, maybe delusions, at least for now," Doc replies, perhaps with a tinge of jovial fascination.

"What have you learned?" the Commander asks Doc.

Doc replies, "This is far outside my wheelhouse. But come...." He leads you all to a bevy of pinned-up x-rays photographs. At first glance, they show a skeleton as expected.

"Look here," he says, pointing to a chest x-ray. "The overall bone structure is normal for a goliath and his cardiac structures are close to normal, but everything else... there's quite a bit of missing, shrunken, or misplaced."

"What?!" Slacks says.

You're mortified. You fear he cannot recover from this.

"Which means?" the Commander asks.

"Don't know. He's alive, not a zombie, thankfully," Doc answers. "But he feels no pain and incisions I make heal rapidly, though they leave scars." He picks up a nearby surgical drill. "This puppy is most effective." By "puppy" he means the drill.

You watch with hope, fascination, and pain as Doc demonstrates by gently drilling into the mage's chest and then the right temple area of his skull. Mancy peers in for a closer look. Olive-colored ooze seeps from the wounds before they close.

Doc explains, "much of his innards, including half of his brain, now consist of this strange protoplasm."

He heads over to a microscope, which straddles over a glass slide smudged with green goo. With the flip of a switch, an attached projector shows the goo in microscopic detail.

The goo slowly slithers and devours a last normal cell.

Mancy declares, "It's bio-mechanical." She reaches over as if to touch it, but decides not to. She sniffs it. "It has the look, smell, and consistency of oil used to lubricate an ergo's innards."

A lump of bile comes to the bottom of your mouth.

Slacks' mouth hangs agog. The Commander is grim.

"Skips like a stone across a pond," the mage babbles.

"Oh, here's some odd scarring," Doc adds, shifting all eyes to geometric lines etched deeply into the skin of the mage's breast.

You recognize it. "It is a sigil, a magic circle" you explain. "It matches what's on Mad Muse." You add silently, *and in the occult book.* It is the sigil of the spirit Doomed Salu'im.

Everyone looks to you.

"Perhaps an *Erase* spell would remove it and end his affliction," you offer impulsively, feeling optimistic.

"Can we do that now?" the Commander asks.

You are about to say 'no' but reconsider. Technically, you don't know that spell. But *what if*, you wonder, you mastered *Erase* over some other spell in school? Maybe you could use the loo mirror to learn how to erase this sigil, assuming last night wasn't some insane nightmare. *It's worth a try*, you reason.

"Um... I must prepare," you reply.

The mage babbles to you, "Mr. Demos Kalagos came, yes?" He tugs as if begging you to acknowledge him. "Ernest?"

"He's out of it," Doc says.

"Hmm," you say, "I feel he's struggling to communicate." You go over and gently take his hand to console him.

"You're still in there, Papa, I know it, and we're going to bring you back to us," you say, determined to figure this out.

TRY AN ACT OF FAITH.
(X=D20 + 3 IF FAITH IS A GIFT.)

YOU FAIL IF X IS LESS THAN 14:

"Liar, liar!" the mage spits out at you. "By needles they fly and with scalpels aim to fix you."

A dizzying wave of grief and pain bludgeons your senses and your knees almost buckle, but the mage's arm reaches out to strongly catch you, preventing you from falling.

By his touch, in a blinding flash, you feel you are back in your childhood kitchen. You mother is baking pie that lazy afternoon just before the devils came. She smiles at you, but her teeth are razor sharp. Her eyes are red. The set of kitchenware at her fingertips includes needles and scalpals.

"Agh!" you yell, trying to push away the terrible vision.

Mage Greene grips tighter. In the vision, Calv Nyquist

stands in a corner staring at you. Of course, he hadn't actually been there that fateful night. *Why is the mage showing you this?*

YOU LOSE 1 VITALITY POINT AND 1 SANITY POINT. YOU MUST TRY AGAIN AND REPEAT THIS SECTION UNTIL YOU SUCCEED.

WHEN YOU SUCCEED:

You catch a flash of Calv Nyquist in your mind's eye.

"Follow him," the mage says. You feel sure he is trying to communicate with you. Then just as suddenly as the vision struck you, it ends and the mage lets go of your arm.

"You okay?" the Commander asks as Mancy steadies you.

"Yessir," you reply. "Bizarre."

"He is our 'gentle bean'," Mancy inserts. "It's hard to see him this way," she adds, trying to explain your reaction.

"But is Greene a danger?" the Commander asks Doc.

The Doc replies, "He's often comatose. Maybe saveable."

The Commander turns to you. "Surely this is disconcerting," he says empathetically. "Now how goes the investigation? Are you finding any answers?"

"He was dabbling in occult magic. He summoned and bound a spirit into Mad Muse, then things went sideways."

"That doesn't sound like him," the Commander replies.

"No, it doesn't," you agree. "Which is why, given... some evidence... I suspect Mr. Nyquist knows more than he's let on.

"Really?" The Commander is intrigued.

"I know he's a civilian, but this is... a dangerous situation. I'd like your permission to interview him."

The Commander considers. "Hmm. That could invite a complaint. Give it a go, but keep it to a nice chat, shall we?"

"Yessir," you reply. "I'll schedule him after Chapel."

GO TO THE NEXT SCENE.

85

Scene #24

Dissonance

Because it's Sunday morning 0900 hours, most airmen are now in Chapel. You and Mancy are in the second row of pews. You are feeling somewhat nauseous but making do.

"Let us pray," the parson says, "notably for our brothers and sisters lost on their way to their families. O Divine Shepherd, may You bring into Your fold our thirteen airmen who passed into the Great Beyond this day. May they rejoice in Your compassionate presence in Your heavenly home."

"May they rest in peace," everyone recites.

You are not strongly religious. No patron appeals to you except Saint Cuthbert, who aids those seeking justice or some say vengeance. The patrons let down your family and many others during the Great War years ago. "Let down" is an understatement. They utterly abandoned you all to devils. And where are the souls of your family member now? Did they and all the rest die to face a worse fate? No one knows.

The parson opens a silvery tome. "Today we read from the Book of Roshar the Burning Prophet, whose deeds and words remind us to trust in the Almighty's unique plan for each of us."

You try your best to pay attention as he reads, though you feel a confusing mix of sleepy, thirsty, and sick to your stomach. You've never suffered a hangover so strong from wine. *Why has no one crafted a spell for mornings like this?* Or maybe someone did but the Royal Council of Wizards keeps it secret?

The parson continues reading: "...the people shouted, 'Roshar, you are wise and mighty. We will follow you!' But Roshar did not think of himself thusly. 'Only the Lord is so,' he schooled them. 'And our journey is far from over.'"

Your mind churns through the morning's events. What befell the dead airman? And Mage Greene clearly has himself in a pickle. You barely hold back your laughter at the odd phrase.

Try an Act of Endurance.
(X=D20 + 3 if Endurance is a Gift.)

You fail if X is less than 9:

Staying quiet takes effort. Singing burns. Praying pains you. You start to sweat profusely.

"... how many times have You given us the strength to just keep..." the parson is saying in the midst of his exegesis. "... up our faith, for we travel as a community...."

Your mind wanders to the chapel's layout. It's a simple stone chamber with a pane of stained glass. There are no icons. The focus is faith and service, not a gaudy show of wealth and power like the ornate cathedrals on the Continent. You remember going there as a tiny boy. The richly robed priests there spoke then in an odd tongue that you know now held words of magic.

"... that would be like wrestling with our shadow..." the parson continues.

You almost retch but burp silently. You're feverish.

You lose 1 vitality and 1 sanity.
You must repeat this scene until you succeed.

When you succeed:

Mancy tightly grasps your hand in warm friendship, and instantly you recover your senses. Despite her tough demeanor and occasional swagger, she can be a solid friend.

You smile at her in thanks.

The parson's tone drops an octave in seriousness. "On this our weekly day of rest and communion, we beseech Our

Holy Lord for a blessing, sign, or wonder."

Everyone kneels in earnest prayer.

The parson prepares an offering of yellow roses, tourmaline stones, motes of diamond dust, and a roll of blue and white silks, all symbols of healing and wards against negative energy.

"O High Creator with Your blessed daughter Esmariah, patron of healing, we the community of Fingal Royal Air Force Base offer up these precious treasures and beseech in all humbleness that You touch our precious servant Mage Radulfr Greene, such that he returns from the brink of death with a clear mind, purified body, and spiritual abundance to continue serving on Your behalf."

With gestures and whispers, the parson completes the offering, the items vanish from the alter, and silence envelopes the room. What boon, if any, will be delivered in exchange? As you know, there are many factors but ultimately the Creator's plan trumps all. Often, nothing special occurs. Just often enough, though, the offering results in an actual miracle.

Silence holds as the parson meditates awaiting a result.

He gasps briefly.

"All rise," he announces as he pulls himself up.

"By infinite wisdom, the Almighty has veiled our home in a mantle of protection from vile forces for the coming week. May we rejoice."

"We rejoice!" everyone shouts.

You are sad that Mage Greene has not been healed, for whatever reason. Though the form of divine intervention suggests a greater danger is yet to come.

The service ends: "Go in peace, and be well one and all."

Everyone heads like a herd of unctuous goats to the mess hall to break their fast. But you're still fairly nauseous and let Mancy and the others know you'll see them later.

"You okay, Lieutenant?" Calv asks as you pass him.

"Not entirely," you answer. "This morning's find was ugly."

GO TO THE NEXT SCENE.

Scene #25

Something is Terribly Wrong

You want to interview Calv but are not feeling well. You need a nap but can't now. Mage Greene can't wait for answers. You'll just quickly freshen up first.

You go to the showers. Perhaps a nice shower will help you. You briefly chat with a pal there, a pilot named Hargrave, and indeed feel better. You return to your quarters.

What if I had that occult book? You wonder. It would probably have a lot more information. Maybe you should go back to town again and visit the old man? The book mentioned nightmares, urges, and black-outs, right? What did the old man say about taint and insanity?

A soldier comes to your quarters and drops off a message. The message is from the office of Dr. Joan Carver. It thanks you for your interest in her work, and informs you that she is on assignment in the jungle ruins of Old Nezembar. It reads in part, "We should be hearing from her any time and will leave a message on your behalf to contact you when she can."

How odd their office replies on a Sunday? Well, it's dated as received last night. But come to think of it, did you even contact them? You can't quite recall. Oh wait, you told Slacks to contact her. Yes, that's it. Your head hurts. My, you're addled!

You put the message into your pocket... there's something extra already in there. *That's odd.* You take out a ring from your pocket. You suddenly recall taking it from your pilot pal, practically minutes ago in the showers. You grabbed it from Hargrave's unattended heap of garments.

Wait, what?! You are aghast that you've stolen something!
Ugh, what's going on?
You go to the loo mirror and stare at yourself.
It ripples to life.
Holy shite!

89

TRY AN ACT OF FAITH.
(X=D20 + 3 IF FAITH IS A GIFT.)

YOU FAIL IF X IS LESS THAN 9:

The mirror shows you yesterday back at the old man's house, reading that book, *Occult Mysteries of the Atlan Empire* by Dr. Joan Carver. You're tracing its sigils with your finger, silently mumbling some of the book's incantations, eager to understand and harness its power. You watch helplessly as you pilfer the book, secreting it under your coat. Then there you are last night in your room, reading it.

YOU LOSE 1D3 SANITY POINTS.
CONTINUE TO SUCCESS.

WHEN YOU SUCCEED:

No, no, no. You flee the loo, slamming the door shut.

You return to your bed and... there's that book, *Occult Mysteries*, lying on the nightstand. It taunts you!

Agh! How did it get here? You didn't steal it! Or did you?

It has a bookmark. As you open to the marked page, you see the bookmark is plainly crafted from tanned human skin. *Ugh!* You toss it aside, disgusted, but cannot resist reading. The page instructs how to conjure the spirit of Doomed Salu'im.

"You need to see the priest, right now," you decide aloud, slamming shut the book. "Get a grip on yourself!"

You exit your quarters, sure to lock the door behind you. And although you can't see through doors or walls like Mind Spy can, you certainly feel the book calling to you.

You gulp hard and hustle down to the Chapel.

GO TO THE NEXT SCENE.

Scene #26

Seeking Absolution

You knock on the parson's door. The door plaque reads, "Minister Archibald Macpherson."

After a moment, the parson answers. "Yes, airman?"

"I am in need of private counsel," you say gravely.

"Of course, come in," he replies as he warmly ushers you into his office. The space is simple wood and stone with a thick rug, three stuffed chairs, a table and bookcase, holy water vials, and minor religious appointments. You two sit face to face a few feet apart. "Perhaps I can ease your distress?" he offers as he closes a second interior door, sound-proofing the room.

"I may need a bit of help" you reply as you absently scan the room, too nervous to start. You recall that as a child, in the Continental cathedral, all the faces of the saints looked down on you from their iconic afterlives. In his room, however, there are no icons. "By the way, I'm Lieutenant Ernest." You extend your hand to shake. He takes your hand and holds it warmly.

"No formalities here," he explains.

You quietly sit face to face, your head feeling tired.

"Perhaps you have some sins to confess?"

"What?" you ask. You haven't sat for confession with someone since you were a boy.

"It's a great way to start, clearing the air and all that."

"Uh, sure." You wonder what to confess. What have you actually done wrong? Some missteps are clear but how much has been of your own volition?

"Your confession is confidential," he explains, "unless it is a major crime such as murder. That I must report."

"Got it, I'll start," you say, still feeling deeply uneasy.

What do you confess? Do you focus on 1)

"Truly, I have sinned," you start. You confess, and as you finish your list of misdeeds, you mention that you are unsure if your actions are due to some weakness of character under pressure, or due to casting a spell beyond your power, or both.

Quietly to yourself, you wonder if Slacks spiked your spell dust. Or maybe that's a convenient excuse, you chide yourself. In any case, you acutely feel that you have done wrong—several wrongs—and surely need atonement.

"I'm curious if you've been feeling ill, why didn't you go to the infirmary?" the parson asks.

Good question, you muse. You don't want the Commander or any of your mates to think you are suffering a crack up, a psychotic break. You would be taken off the case and perhaps hauled off to an asylum. *Best not to say that!*

"This occult spirit stuff, it has a touch of evil," you reply. "I can feel it."

"It's good to hear that you've named it and come to the right place. Dispelling evil is my mainstay."

"So what do we do?" you ask.

"Let us kneel on the floor," he explains.

You two kneel. Happily, the rug is thick and comfortable.

"Know this chamber is soundproofed to contain whatever happens. Just say or do whatever you must."

"Yessir."

You two pray together, and then the parson rises, applies a drop of holy oil to your forehead, and chants over you. As he chants, he moves his hands over your body, sweeping his arms in and out as if pulling weeds from a garden or snakes by their heads from their hiding holes.

TRY AN ACT OF FAITH.
(X=D20 + 3 IF FAITH IS A GIFT.
ADD +2 IF YOU FOCUS ON MISUSE OF MAGIC.)

You fail if X is less than 9:

You begin to shake, first lightly and then all over. You've been holding your breath. Now you gasp for air, and as you do, you cough violently, over and other, as if forcibly expelling demons. Your eyes fill with tears from the coughing and from a sense of loss.

You burst with tears. Your dead parents, family, and friends, the terror of the devils, the loneliness growing up at the base, the lack… the challenge of always staying strong.

"And I tried to hide, but I was caught, and the devils injected me with something, to make me one of them…" Even as you finally say the words aloud, a great relief washes over you.

"The room is soundproof," he reminds you.

You scream and scream again until you collapse into a ball in a violent coughing fit followed by more tears.

The parson stands back and chants again. Among the strange words, he invokes for you a blessing.

You lose 1 vitality point.
Continue to success.

When you succeed:

You sob for a few minutes, then slowly dry your eyes.

The parson hands you a kerchief. "Good job," he soothes as you rise and slump in the chair, exhausted and sad but also overall feeling much better. Your mushy head, heavy chest, and sickened stomach all return to normal.

The two of you sit quietly. A clock ticks in the background. "What was all that?" you ask finally.

"You were tainted by evil. It was starting to have you in

its grip. Truly, no kidding."

"Thank you, Minister."

"Child, let us thank the Creator."

Before you leave, the parson says: "Whatever you are working with, take care—more than a bit of care, mind you— because if only a day has passed in contact with this vile magic, or whatever it is, and here you are, your soul is truly in danger."

"Understood."

He adds, "If you feel any need… uh, actually in two days, I will inquire with the Commander for you to visit me again if you haven't already." He smiles warmly.

You make a mental note to return.

"Wait, here," he says, as he takes from his desk a jade cross on a gold chain. "Wear this, to protect you from whatever evil you face in the coming days." He places it around your neck and you tuck it under your shirt.

You feel warm with gratitude.

"I'm sorry that I tend to miss services," you say.

"The Creator understands," he replies. "That said, having a regular spiritual practice is important. How often are you giving thanks at meals or praying in your quarters?"

"I'm not, to be frank," you reply. "It doesn't come easily."

"You've felt angry and hurt," he says.

You consider for a moment. "Quite right."

"Each and all of us are called to find our own best way. Keep working toward honest goodness. Today is a bit of that." He gives a gentle laugh. "Getting rest might also help."

"If only *that* came more easily too..."

You make to go.

"Special Lieutenant, you have earned your responsibilities, your *ability* to *respond*. We all face things in good time, and perhaps today is shaping up to be that time."

YOU RECOVER 10 SANITY POINTS AND 10 VITALITY POINTS (LIMITED TO YOUR NORMAL MAXIMUM). GO TO THE NEXT SCENE.

PART VII

TRUTH, LIES & TURBULENCE

SCENE #27

TAKING OFF THE MASK

You have a hunch. The one person with whom you are unfamiliar is Calv Nyquist. He is a recent visitor and Mage Greene, even with his scrambled brain, gave you a vision of him. Perhaps his arrival and the spellship's deadly voyage are actually related? What is in that box of his anyway? You can summon him to submit to a lie detector test.

Finally feeling solid and sane, you issue a summons. Soon after, military police usher Calv into the small bunker-like room that holds chairs and a table with a polygraph machine.

"This is awkward," Calv says as the police sit him down and exit to wait just outside.

"It's just a hunch," you say. "A hunch before lunch."

"Okay then," he replies. His left eye twitches a little.

As you hook up the polygraph, you summarize his legal rights and how the process works.

HOW DO YOU CONDUCT THE SESSION? ARE YOU MORE 1) AGGRESSIVE, 2) CURIOUS, 3) NAIVE, 4) PERSONAL, OR 5) SERIOUS?

"Please state your name," you say.

"Calvin Bertrand Nyquist," he replies. The polygraph's needle stays calm, indicating he speaks the truth.

"Where were you born?" you ask.

"Republique du Gaul, in Parnesee." That's true too.

"Nyquist is not a local surname there," you point out.

"My paternal grandfather, a Nyquist, is from the Vikin-landir Freestates." The polygraph confirms that as truthful.

"What is your date of birth?" you ask.

"The first day of the year," he answers honestly.

"Humph, somebody must be born that day. What year?"

"1899," he answers quickly. The polygraph reports inconclusive. You wonder, do men too lie about their age? He looks like he's in his mid-thirties. But perhaps he consumes enough spell dust to truly hold back the years?

"Do you consider yourself vain?" you prod him.

"Not at all," he replies. The polygraph dances wildly, indicating a lie. He smirks as if toying with you.

"And who is your ultimate employer?" you ask.

"That would be His Majesty King George V, under the auspices of the Society of the Royal Cabinet." The polygraph gently confirms that as true.

You are vaguely familiar with Royal Cabinet. It is a division of the civil service that tracks and removes magical and monstrous dangers at large for the whole Commonweal and its allies. You have questions but it's time for the main course.

"What's in the box?"

Calv does not answer.

TRY AN ACT OF CHARM.
(X=D20 + 3 IF CHARM IS A GIFT.
ADD +2 IF YOU ARE PERSONAL.)

———————————————

YOU FAIL IF X IS LESS THAN 9:

"Why did you bring the box?" you ask, rephrasing.

"Are you sure you want to know the answer?" he asks.

"Yes," you reply, adamant.

Calv replies. "The box isn't what needs your attention, and once you hear the answer, you can't un-hear it."

You stop to consider what Mage Greene would suggest. He likes to say that knowledge is always better than ignorance, but he has also said that knowledge can easily corrupt. He would also vouch for helping as many other people as possible.

"I need to do my job, Mr. Nyquist, for everyone's sake, especially if some greater danger, *evil,* is headed here."

With the word *evil*, something stirs in your stomach, pushing up a vile aftertaste. Your brow breaks out with sweat. You suddenly feel as if you're climbing a sheer wall of rock and have taken a perilous route up and may fall.

"That's noble of you," Calv offers, honestly. "Uh, are you okay?" he asks with genuine concern.

You regain your composure and straighten up.

"Please tell me, what's in the box you brought to base?"

YOU LOSE 1 SANITY POINT.
CONTINUE TO SUCCESS.

WHEN YOU SUCCEED:

"It's called a magic resonating catalyst, or meerkat."

"Go on." You prod him.

"It's used to amplify any and all magical potentials within a wide area, roughly 120 feet around it."

The polygraph affirms his words but many questions swirl in your head. You zero in on one: "What do you mean, potentials?"

"Magic works a bit like electrotech. It flows along gradients. The meerkat steepens the slope of those gradients." You guess he means magic will behave in a more extreme way.

"The box is lead-lined," you point out. "Magic doesn't work through lead."

"Actually, not quite. The box's thin lead straps are placed strategically to disguise its purpose while subtly modulating its effects." He explains this with pride. The polygraph says true.

Hmm, you wonder. What if the box was actually the cause of your bizarre magical time-shifting using your mirror, not to mention the spellship mishap? And did this box drive Mage Greene to gooey madness?

"Why did you bring the box here?" you ask.

GO TO THE NEXT SCENE.

Scene #28

Unlikely and Not Assured

Calv hesitates, then slowly answers: "I brought the box at the behest of Royal Cabinet to activate... the next hierian." The polygraph reports his answer is true.

Hierians: Not just comic book fictions, but the world's real superheroes. You wonder who that next hierian is. *Oh...*

HOW DO YOU PROCEED? ARE YOU MORE
1) SKEPTICAL, 2) EXCITED LIKE A KID, 3) CONCERNED
FOR THE FUTURE, 4) CURIOUS, OR 5) ANGRY THAT
SO MANY HAVE SUFFERED AND DIED FOR THIS?

Calv adds, "We're not to toy with the process but..."

"I'm a super he-... an heirian?" you interrupt. "I can't be. I mean, do you, uh, do you believe I'm that hierian?!"

"That's looking more likely," Calv answers.

You give him a look of disbelief. He must be joking.

He explains, "It's a matter of probabilities. Perhaps you've heard of Quantum Mechanics?"

You have a vague sense of what he's referring to but also feel out of your depth. "Did you know in advance?" you ask.

"No. We just got a tip, a prophecy if you will, that some-one *here* had potential." The polygraph reports truth.

You sit and take it all in. Questions flood your mind. "What am I to do? What happens next? I mean, I've read in the comics... Mind Spy's story is..."

"There are responsibilities." He grins. "We would like you to join Cabinet, if not now then in good time."

"Do I get a title, like Mind Spy?" you ask jokingly.

He laughs. "I can't guarantee anyone will call you by it."

This still strikes you as unbelievable.

"Don't all hierians fly or is that just in the comics?"

Calv chuckles. The polygraph needle darts about.

"Listen," you emphasize, "my friend and mentor Mage Greene is scrambled like eggs right now. How can we save him?"

"Can't help with that," he replies.

"Like the Nine Hells!" you snap, angry. "You caused this. You'll help or at least tell me what to do." Alas, the polygraph can't make him speak answers, and maneuvering him to actually help you will take a bit of smart thinking.

He sits impassively, just blinking.

TRY AN ACT OF INTELLECT.
(X=D20 + 3 IF INTELLECT IS A GIFT.
ADD +2 IF YOU CHOSE THE CURIOUS OPTION.
ADD +5 IF YOU HAVE THE "MIND SPY CLUE".)

———————————————

YOU FAIL IF X IS LESS THAN 17:

In a strong voice, you ask, "Are you able to cooperate?"

"Little more than I have," Calv says nonchalantly, "unless you find a way to bend me." He smiles slyly as if to rile you up.

"Why not?" you ask, incredulous.

"I could say helping you is not in my interest. But that's not it. It's legalities, protocol, and all that. Don't want to get disciplined or sacked. Honestly, I like you and wish you the best."

"So kind," you reply sarcastically even as the polygraph again says he's being honest.

"You'll see," Calv replies coolly. "Probably. I'm in for you."

You feel nauseous as if you're at your loo mirror again. You push away that feeling and focus. What would Mage Greene do? *Turn it around!* is what he would advise. Maybe the trick is to let Calv feel in control and question you? You pause for effect. "Sorry, I'm feeling a bit dizzy," you say.

YOU LOSE 1 SANITY POINT.
YOU MUST KEEP TRYING UNTIL YOU SUCCEED.

WHEN YOU SUCCEED:

"Listen," Calv says, "I have a question for you.

"Yes?" you ask, feigning a weak voice.

"I can turn off the box. Do you want that?"

At first, you think *yes*, as that will surely save Mage Greene. But would it? "What will happen?" you ask.

"Likely, your new-found power will fade, whatever it is."

"And Mage Greene's fate?"

"He will pass on in a more natural, painless death."

You wonder if you can reach back in time and convince Mage Greene to not get on the spellship.

He continues earnestly, "We cannot change fate, but we can change how we meet those fixed points in time."

You wonder if he knows about your mirror power. Right now, there's no time for that. Better to focus on what's next.

"There's some kind of monster lurking about or coming, isn't there?" you surmise. "Another ghostly spirit or what?"

"You're on the right path," he replies, evasive but nodding his head. "You impress me, Special Lieutenant."

"No doubt," you reply, annoyed. "Wait, why did you put the box on the spellship yesterday morning?"

"It was turned on for a full week here with no result. I figured the intel we got was a mistake and it was time to move on." The polygraph confirms his honesty.

"Ok. So how can we protect ourselves?" you ask.

"Jade helps," he replies.

"Good to know. And..." You urge him to say more.

"How about we help each other?" he offers. "You know, you give a little, I give more."

"I'm guessing there's a bit in this for you?" you reply.

"I could use your help with a small job in town," he explains. "It's some recon. It would be an in and out job."

"Yeah, I don't trust you," you reply. "That box of yours

basically killed people I care about and has endangered more."

Your honesty quiets him. After a moment of reflection, he replies. "Fair enough. You're angry."

"I'm heartbroken and not that stupid," you reply. "This better be brilliant."

"We'll see if you can handle it," he replies, baiting you.

IF YOU IGNORE CALV'S OFFER AND GO DO RESEARCH ON YOUR OWN, GO SCENE #31 (PAGE 108). OR, TO HEAR HIM OUT, CONTINUE BELOW.

"Tell me more," you say.

"New intel says a potential fugitive from the Continent has settled here in this town. Apparently, she eluded a seasoned investigator and came here a few months ago, gathering allies. We believe she's a turncoat and an occultist."

"And?" You sense he's leaving out something important.

"And I'm guessing she's the individual who actually sold Mage Greene those occult materials and gave him guidance."

"Sounds nasty. Why not bring in your Cabinet chums?"

"They'll recognize us. Thus, maybe you can do recon."

"I'd need authorization," you object.

"I authorize you." He chuckles. "In all seriousness, the Commander gives his okay." You figure if the Commander approves, then it's something he may want you to do.

"Okay," you say. What do you have in mind?"

"There's a magic shop in town called Mikka's Marvels or something like that."

"Madame Mikka's. I've seen it. It's new."

"Pick up some spell dust and ask about pactmaking. Ask really quietly. The clerk may give you a lead to Mikka, or more."

You consider. Even if you continue with Calv's help, you need premium spell dust, and that shop surely carries some.

GO TO THE NEXT SCENE.

Scene #29

Magic Shop

In the morning, you head to Madame Mikka's. It's the magic shop on Parade Street that you spotted earlier. Happily, the street is free of ruffians in these early hours.

You try the shop's door, but it resists. The woman inside at the counter keeps busy, oblivious to your attempt.

"*Patefacio!*" you utter with a wave, affording entry. The shop is exclusive to spellcasters. That would be you. You smile.

A nearby doll announces, "Welcome wizard!"

The shop is artistically decked out, almost plush, and stocked high to the ceiling with all manner of books, from pocket scrolls to ironclad tomes, along with spell ingredients in snazzy bottles and oak boxes, and oddities such as a rusted sign in a corner that reads "Tina's Bookstore and Cematorium". Many items sports motifs of blood, the moon and night, and women. You spot a candle with an occult sigil.

As you peruse the aisles, you rub the amulet around your neck. "*Fateor,*" you whisper. It causes any and all magical items or such within fifteen feet to glow. Sure enough, several items glow. Mostly, they are on display behind glass at the sales counter, under the nose of its lovely but impassive proprietor.

"Any trinkets catch your eye?" she asks cooly.

Your mind rummages around searching for a way to ask for premium spell dust. After all, you might want to cast "Point the Way" or something like it again.

You saunter up to the counter.

"Charming shop," you say. "Do you handle... special orders?" You hope she gets the hint.

TRY AN ACT OF CHARM.
(X=D20 + 3 IF CHARM IS A GIFT.)

You fail if X is less than 15:

"Perhaps," she replies all business-like. "You ought to talk to the owner." She hands you a small gold-inked card that looks more like a dinner invitation than a business card.

"Excellent, thank you." You pocket it.

You loiter briefly in awkward silence. Now you realize why so many people just stand around awkwardly on this street. Everyone is trying to get something illegal or secret. You consider, *perhaps I should buy something?*

You must try again. For each 1 coin you spend before rolling, apply a +1 bonus to your roll. Keep trying until you succeed.

When you succeed:

"Do you have more of this candle," you ask, referring to the one with the occult sigil. "Or items like it...."

"You know Mr. Demos Kalagos?" she asks, testing you. You vaguely recall the old man mentioning that spirit.

"I don't know... that spirit," you answer carefully. "I'm thinking more along the lines of Mr. Salu'im."

"Oh!" she exclaims. She warms up considerably. "You've come to the right place. You just wait right here."

She vanishes into a back room behind a colorful curtain. As you wait, you scan the shop. A clock ticks. Perhaps some of the dolls are watching you?

She returns with a vial of premium spell dust along with a letter. "Ten sterling," she says. "And the letter is free."

As you exit, you feel that was all too easy.

You gain an invitation to dine with "Madam Mikka". The address is the in Capitol city, Londimium. Go to the next scene.

Scene #30

Look But Don't Touch

Back at base, you debrief Calv in his quarters on your trip to Mikka's magic shop. He pours tea as you two sit.

"That was suspiciously easy," you say as you show him the invitation you received.

"Excellent! Tell me everything," he encourages you.

Fortunately, you have an excellent memory for details, and he scribbles your verbal debrief in a notebook.

"I have an idea," he offers as you finish. "I'm betting you can look back in time and start to shift events without actually settling on a change. What if... you tried taking books, searching behind the counter, asking off-beat questions...."

"So lying and stealing? you ask, scornful but intrigued.

"More like withdrawing from sex at the last bump," he says.

You laugh at the analogy but also feel uncomfortable.

"You're definitely special," he offers. "I'm just guessing, taking an educated stab in the dark. It's worth a try, right?"

"I haven't seen you use any magic," you say. You wonder, is he an *hierian* too, a superhero with his own power?

"I'm not magical, just awesome," he replies cheekily.

You stand to go. "Ok. I'll try your idea and let you know."

"You can do it here," he offers, "whatever it is you do. Or not. I won't judge. I can give you some support as you go."

You recall something Mage Greene once said: *When someone's extra eager to help, they've likely done it before.* "Recruiting is your job, your magic, isn't it?" you ask.

"Yes." He smiles. "And like you, I'm still figuring it out."

"Okay then." You agree to time-shift with him next to you. "I'll need a mirror," you explain. "And a lot of spell dust."

He gets you a mirror, and you unpocket some dust.

You sit and focus intensely on the mirror.

Once ready, you rewind back in the mirror to the shop.

Demos Kalagos
Sworn Enemy of Time

Preparations: Firstly, draw Demos Kalagos's seal while an item worth at least 250 gold coins sits nearby. You must have stolen the item from a foe. The spirit responds well if you are a gnome, kobold, or puzzle master. Alternatively, you must be able to cast at least ten different spells. Finally, as you gaze into a mirror and chant, you watch yourself age from infant to child, adolescent to adult, middle-aged to old but no more, denying the moment of actual death.

Legend: Demos Kalagos is friendly with his summoners. Gregarious and fond of interviews, he spins stories of his exploits to those who question him, though sages say most of his stories are easily falsified. Whatever the case, Demos claims he was once a mortal gnome trickster, renowned for having fooled the cosmic forces of Death and Magic. Then one day, he tried to trick the cosmic force of Time to prove his skills. He succeeded, stealing power over time itself for a single day. But what he didn't realize is that an infinite number of himself existed across an infinite number of timelines. Thus, when he stepped into Time's realm, an infinite number of other Demoses followed him, and one had prepared a trap that erased the others from reality forever by caging them within the Spirit Realm. Occult scholars deny this legend, as Time is not a conscious entity. They say perhaps Demos was simply insane.

Powers: Demos Kalagos aids you to alter, resist, or analyze time's flow. Once daily, you can look into a mirror, rewind to a past point in your life, and alter a minor choice you made. He allows you to resist or join the temporal movement of others, and he aids making traps and performing amusing tricks. Finally, up to thrice in your life, you may permanently rewind your visible age by ten years.

TRY AN ACT OF ENDURANCE.
(X=D20 + 3 IF ENDURANCE IS A GIFT.)

YOU FAIL IF X IS LESS THAN 15:

Resisting the allure to make brute changes to the time line quickly proves exhausting. You violently back off at times, letting a memory recede, then relax to try again.

YOU EXPEND 1D6 VITALITY AND 1 SANITY POINT. REPEAT THIS SECTION UNTIL YOU SUCCEED.

WHEN YOU SUCCEED, TRY A 2ND ACT OF ENDURANCE AS ABOVE, THEN WHEN YOU RETURN HERE, TRY A 3RD ACT UNTIL YOU GATHER 3 SECRETS TOTAL.

Success! You learn three secrets. First, you "half steal" a tiny black book about another time-bending spirit called Demos Kalagos. Oddly, the powers that spirit grants are just like yours! It's surely not by chance. How or why are you like a spirit you've never heard of? Second, you "half find" a letter with a specific mailing address for Mikka in the Commonweal's capital city, Londimium. Third, you "half lie" about your past and power to figure out that Mikka and her ilk are surely vampires.

"Wow, that's amazing!" you exclaim, finishing up.

"Yes, you're a wonder," Calv replies.

YOU GAIN A BOON. LATER IN THE GAME, YOU CAN USE IT TO GAIN A +5 BONUS TO A SINGLE D20 ROLL.

TO STAY WITH CALV, GO TO SCENE #32A (PAGE 111).
TO VISIT MANCY, GO TO SCENE #32B (PAGE 115).
OR TO VISIT SLACKS, GO TO SCENE #32C (PAGE 118).
ALL THREE INCLUDE AN OPTION FOR ROMANCE.

Scene #31

Know Thy Limits

It's night, 1930 hours. Your head spins with questions. Where a different course of events until now even possible? *What if...* In your quarters, you use the loo mirror to fiddle with the past. In Mage Greene's place, could you have boarded the spellship? Or at least prevented him from boarding? Before taking drastic measures, now might be the best time to test the limits of your power and hopefully answer these questions.

How do you approach experimenting? Do you 1) tiptoe cautiously with trifling changes, 2) Push with passion for an exciting change, or 3) Pray for guidance and consider what Mage Greene would suggest?

You wonder whether using this power is wise. Should you even try to alter events? Maybe the answer depends on how much more happiness would come with a change, to feel better or do better in life in some way? What if a change brought happiness to some and misery to others? In your experience, small changes can usher in meaningful improvements.

After some trepidation, you get started, searching in the mirror for ways to retroactively save Mage Greene.

Try an Act of Endurance. (X=D20 + 3 if Endurance is a gift. Apply +2 bonus if make trifling changes or consider what Mage Greene would do.)

You fail if X is less than 15:

You question yourself and feel distracted. With what kind of magic are you playing? Will you become misguided like Mage Greene and harm yourself or perhaps others? Who or what are you anyway? *Indeed, what kind of person sifts through alternate realities to swap out solid facts for new and different?*

You think back to when you were accepted to attend Command School. You felt a jumble of doubts then too. To ease your mind, you asked Mage Greene, "Maybe I should get more experience here first and wait a few years?"

"Aw, lad, you're better than that," he replied, adding his usual warm smile. "I've got faith you can handle it."

After that, you got up the courage to tell your mates that you tested "true" for magic. They roused you to go off and make more of yourself. You did, and that was three years ago.

With that comforting memory, you try various options, going through them systematically as Mage Greene once demonstrated when you two solved a puzzle together.

YOU EXPEND 1D6 VITALITY AND 1 SANITY POINT. REPEAT THIS SECTION UNTIL YOU SUCCEED.

WHEN YOU SUCCEED:

After great frustration, but also with modest relief, you find that much of what you try doesn't work.

You figure out several points. Firstly, you must personally be at the targeted moment in time. Also, your choices must generally be small, recent, and specific such as re-choosing what you ate this morning or what you focused on learning in a lesson. There are a few exceptions, like who you dated. Perhaps there are fixed points, events that cannot change, and also rare flex points, larger events that you can change. Finally, you discover that any reflective surface works, not just your loo mirror.

At first, the lack of success is sad. On the other hand,

you recall Mage Greene once said that knowing a spell's limits is just as crucial as knowing its potential. You smile at recalling his wise words.

YOU GAIN A BOON. LATER IN THE GAME, YOU CAN USE IT TO GAIN A +5 BONUS TO A SINGLE D20 ROLL.

You consider going to bed to rest up. After all, you will be doing your level best tomorrow to help Mage Greene! You turn down your bed, turn off the lights, and rest your head on your pillow. Alas, your eyes refuse to shut. Your mind is simply too turbulent from all of your experimenting.

Perhaps visiting a friend is what I need now? you muse. Or visiting Calv might give you more insights. Whoever you visit, companionship will likely lend you morale.

TO VISIT CALV, GO TO SCENE #32A (PAGE 111).
OR TO VISIT MANCY, GO TO SCENE #32B (PAGE 115).
OR TO VISIT SLACKS, GO TO SCENE #32C (PAGE 118).
ALL THREE INCLUDE AN OPTION FOR ROMANCE.

Scene #32A

Relax With Calv

You relax with Calv in his visitor's quarters over wine. Initially, you're there to chat but perhaps something more will evolve? You know he likes talking about business and travel.

How do you build rapport?
Do you rely more on 1) witty banter, 2) bravado, 3) coyness, 4) caring, 5) curiosity, 6) vulnerability, or 7) being yourself.

"You probably know all my details," you say. "Doesn't the Royal Cabinet hold a file on everyone?" You feel at a disadvantage and wish Calv would share more about himself.

He shrugs. "How could we catalog everyone? Though higher-ups have that on their wishlist. Of course, you're a refugee and an Air Force officer. Your file's a hefty one."

"I remember the day a prim gal came from the Royal Academy of Magic to officially test me for magic potential."

"Yeah, your file opens doors too," Calv explains.

"It was frightening. She subjected me to tests. I secretly hoped I wouldn't have talent because... as you may know."

"You suffered some unpleasantness in your youth."

"Yes." You feel vulnerable. If only he would open up too.

Try an Act of Charm.
(X=D20 + 3 if Charm is a gift. Add +2 if you rely on curiosity or being yourself.)

Option: You can improve your result by casting a Charm spell. If so, spend 1 vitality point now to add +2 more your D20 roll.

Calv asks you a question. "In the area of the base where you faced off with the monster, why is it called 'The Nest'?"

You explain: "It's the oldest section, built on a low hill that was, according to local legend, a nest for a family of griffons centuries ago. Thus the name of town's brothel, Mount Griffon."

Calv laughs.

"I've never seen a griffon," you say. "I hear some remain in the elven isles to the west. I'd love to visit them someday."

"There are dozens of griffons, a breeding stock, at an industrialist's racing stables outside of Scunthorpe," Calv says. "Just mention my name to Mr. Will Lysaght's assistant to enjoy a tour. The whole city's quite a sight now."

"I read about the sky rocks there," you say.

"Yes indeed, whole mansions and their gardens float in the sky on their own private chunks of rock!"

"With so many in poverty, it feels like a waste of magic."

"There's a greater cause. If and when war comes again, we'll be able to move whole facilities and bases through the sky."

"Wow, that would terrify one's foes for sure!"

He chuckles. "No worries, our enemies have theirs too."

You visualize a face-off between two flying fortresses.

"There's a price, no doubt," he adds. "Scunthorpe is heavily industrialized, replete with smog, slag, and ghuls."

"What're ghuls?" you ask. Maybe *seagulls?* You feel naive.

"They're mutants of sorts who banded together after a slight nucleonic accident there. They're punkish boffins."

"Sounds awful."

"They make do. One of my besties is a ghul."

"You must have buckets of friends," you say, "all over the Commonweal." You wonder how important you actually are.

"I call most people acquaintances, and yeah, I keep up some contacts beyond the Commonweal too."

"Even Nymeria?" you ask, referring to a far off desert

empire you've read about where genies run whole cities.

"Not yet," he replies. "Listen, I'll take you griffon riding if we ever get to Scunthorpe."

You nod with enthusiasm, "I'll take you up on the offer."

And then, in a moment of opportunity, when Calv reaches to refill your wine glasses, you can cast a Charm spell.

YOU MUST KEEP CHECKING UNTIL YOU SUCCEED. YOU MAY CAST CHARM AGAIN FOR 1 VITALITY.

WHEN YOU SUCCEED:

YOU MAY STOP HERE AND GO TO BED. IF SO, YOU HEAL 20 VITALITY AND GO TO SCENE #33 (PAGE 121). OTHERWISE, FOR ROMANCE, CONTINUE BELOW.

"Are you familiar with fey ecstacy?" he asks, pulling out a small glass vial. "Bought it off of an elf, not just black market." He sniffs some. His eyes briefly roll back.

"With regards, I'll pass," you say.

Actually, three days from now, you will change your mind and instead you now say, "Just a whiff, thank you."

As the purple smoke lightens your mood, Calv kisses you. Quickly, the action gets heavy and he possesses you with great endurance. Two hours later, you lie in his arms.

Calv quietly tells you the legend of Ghato'Kacha, an occult spirit of good morals that opposes Doomed Salu'im and other evil spirits. The legend sounds very personal to him.

"I'll be easier on you next time," he comments as you go.

YOU SLEEP DEEPLY AND HEAL 30 VITALITY POINTS, EVEN THOUGH YOU GO TO BED LATE!

GO TO SCENE #33 (PAGE 121).

Ghato'Kacha
The Gentle Fiend

Preparations: First, draw Ghato' Kacha's seal, ideally just before sunrise. You must show you understand the eternal birth and death cycle of reincarnation and your place in it. The spirit responds well if you are a yasha, physically strong, or good of heart. Finally, bathe a silver hammer in holy water to banish evil spirits. Soon the hammer will glow like "the longtime sun" as it drips red with blood. As you pull the hammer from the basin, Ghato'Kacha's feline reflection appears within the holy water.

Legend: Ghato'Kacha lived many incarnations and continues on as a spirit to fight evil. According to legend, creatures called yashas are occasionally born from the unions of mortals and rakshasas, which are a fiendish race of tiger spirits. Ghato'Kacha was one such offspring. He was benevolent to all even when first opening his eyes at birth. As a young man, he swore an oath to slay his wicked rakshasa mother for the suffering he saw her inflict on mortals. He succeeded, but she simply reincarnated and continued terrorizing mortals and struck back at him. As Ghato'Kacha lay dying, he pleaded that God give him another life to battle evil anew. The gods agreed. Over centuries of incarnations, Ghato'Kacha feuded with his mother and others of her deceitful race. Then one day while battling atop a volcano, he sealed his victory by stunning his mother with a kiss of true love before hurling them both into molten lava, never to incarnate again.

Powers: Ghato'Kacha aids you in overcoming evil by using a foe's own power against it. Up to five times daily, after an evil foe strikes you, you may automatically inflict identical harm to it. He also helps you influence others through your laughs, smiles, kisses, and caresses. Finally, this spirit physically fortifies you, especially against arrows and bullets, and helps you detect evil creatures.

Scene #32B

Dance with Mancy

You visit Mancy in her quarters. She takes your jacket. Tonight's informal. Initially, you're there to chat and relax but perhaps something more will evolve. You know she likes talking about robots and combat tactics.

How do you build rapport?
Do you rely more on 1) witty banter, 2) bravado, 3) coyness, 4) caring, 5) curiosity, 6) vulnerability, or 7) being yourself.

Mancy pulls out a suitcase, which she opens up to reveal a record player. She puts on a record and turns up the volume a tad louder than is likely regulation. It's a popish jazz tune.

"Heaven... I'm in heaven," the male singer croons, "And my heart beats so that I can hardly speak."

"It's Irving Berlin and Fred Astaire," she says cheerfully. You wouldn't know she had witnessed death two days before.

"And I seem to find the happiness I seek," the song continues. "When we're out together dancing cheek to cheek."

"Come dance with me," she beckons. "I need the practice or all I'll be left knowing are tallywacker morning drills."

You dance with her to *Cheek to Cheek*.

Try an Act of Charm.
(X=D20 + 3 if Charm is a gift. Add +2 if you rely on caring or being yourself.)

Option: You can improve your result by casting a Charm spell. If so, spend 1 vitality point now to add +2 more your D20 roll.

YOU FAIL IF X IS LESS THAN 15:

Mancy chats up a storm. She's in the middle of detailing her favorite ergo, an E-35 model, in the Commonweal's red, white, and blue stars and crosses. She wants in on an upcoming tactical training course. And there's a new trainee mechanic.

"Super cute bum," she says and bites her lip.

Now and then she puts on a new record. She expounds on each song from the fun *Lullaby of Broadway*, sung in an odd accent, to the lazy *Red Sails in the Sunset*.

YOU MUST KEEP CHECKING UNTIL YOU SUCCEED. YOU MAY USE CHARM AGAIN EACH TIME.

WHEN YOU SUCCEED:

"You're sweat, C," Mancy beams.

"I try my best," you reply awkwardly. You like her, but things can get complicated quickly. "And you're the wicked one."

"Ha!" She rejects your compliment. "I'm just a coal country girl who loves airplanes, ergoes and show tunes, a girl who doesn't want to ever marry or pop out *bairns* so she'll be free to live life on her terms." She adds flippantly, "Or something like that."

You understand. The glittering modern age of bright lights and big cities comes with smoke stack poverty, war's ghosts, and tired prejudices. For many, life is a dog's rear end.

"So I'm here, out by lovely moors, fixing broken tech and searching for lost sheep." She laughs, adding, "with you."

YOU MAY STOP HERE AND GO TO BED. IF SO, YOU HEAL 20 VITALITY POINTS AND GO TO SCENE #33 (PAGE 121).

OTHERWISE, FOR ROMANCE, CONTINUE BELOW.

You kiss her softly. She invites you to continue. You two get more comfortable as you explore and provide each other warmth. But then the current record ends and she stops.

She lies back and relaxes, looking up at the ceiling. Only now do you see she's detailed it lightly with all her favorite gizmos on distant and strange planets.

"Not so regulation, is it?" she comments on it.

"It's a beautiful adventure," you reply. "We need dreams."

"We're all gutted, you know, C," she says. "But you're going to be ship-shape, I just know it. You know your onions."

"It doesn't feel that way, not yet." Death and uncertainty has struck you hard. You turn and stare at her. Maybe a kiss?

"I'm truly into you, C, but I can't jeopardize my job," she explains. "I've kept up a spotless record, somehow. I'll give no reason for some prat to deny me a promotion into a pilot's seat."

You understand. In fact, Mage Greene comes to mind. You worry. Is he suffering right now down in the infirmary? Will you be able to save him?

"Let's fall asleep together," she offers. "Dreaming of stars."

"Can I take a rain check?" you reply.

"Yessir, Special Lieuy."

You two laugh and she tosses you off her bed.

YOU SLEEP DEEPLY AND HEAL 30 VITALITY POINTS!

GO TO SCENE #33 (PAGE 121).

Scene #32C

Drink with Slacks

You visit Slacks in his quarters. He takes your jacket. Tonight's informal. Initially, you're there to chat and relax but perhaps something more will evolve. You know he likes talking about history and politics.

How do you build rapport?
Do you rely more on 1) witty banter,
2) bravado, 3) coyness, 4) caring, 5) curiosity,
6) vulnerability, or 7) being yourself.

"What's your poison, C?" he asks. "Gin and Tonic? Maybe a Pimm's or a Regent's Punch?" He fishes for a key from his pocket. "Oh, nix the Pimm's. Got a cucumber but no lemonade."

"Let's see you mix a Regent's," you answer. "It's perfect for a chilly night." You look around but spot no alcohol.

"Excellent choice, sir," he says in a faux servant's accent.

He puts on an electric kettle, clears his desk, and unlocks a cabinet, revealing a bevy of essential spirits. He pulls out champagne, brandy, rum, arrack, and other little bottles with what you assume include such necessities as pineapple syrup. Plainly, the cabinet is larger on the inside than the outside.

"I'm impressed," you say.

"And you haven't even tasted my magic yet," he replies.

You laugh at the entendre.

The water boils and with a flourish over a bucket, he intones, "*Placere misce!*" He winks at you. "What use is a wizard," he opines, "with no magic to mix the perfect drink!"

"You have a spell to cure hangovers too?" you ask.

"What would be the fun in that?" he replies with snark.

He shakes the mixer and pours from it. You two toast,

"Cheers!" and drink down your cups.

"Tasty!" you commend him. "And strong!"

He turns on the radio. "Let's find a good tune to drink to." He searches in vain. "Damn, no classics on tonight."

Briefly, he goes silent, as if going off to a memory. There you see he witnessed death two days before.

TRY AN ACT OF CHARM.
(X=D20 + 3 IF CHARM IS A GIFT. ADD +2 IF YOU RELY ON WITTY BANDER OR BEING YOURSELF.)

OPTION: YOU CAN IMPROVE YOUR RESULT BY CASTING A CHARM SPELL. IF SO, SPEND 1 VITALITY POINT NOW TO ADD +2 MORE YOUR D20 ROLL.

YOU FAIL IF X IS LESS THAN 15:

As you two drink and vainly spout some half-remembered songs, you try to get to something more personal. But he keeps things light, or he adds his usual bluster and swagger whenever you probe.

YOU LOSE 2 VITALITY POINTS FROM HEAVY DRINKING. YOU MUST KEEP TRYING UNTIL YOU SUCCEED. YOU MAY USE CHARM AGAIN EACH TIME.

WHEN YOU SUCCEED:

"Your repertoire of spells is impressive," you say. "Flinging fireballs, your extra-dimensional chest... ventriloquism."

He smiles at that last one. "I can summon a weasel too."

You two laugh.

"So why did you transfer here?" you ask seriously.

"I was reassigned. After pilot school, I trained as a warmage. Once on the ground, one must be combat ready. But that letter you found on me isn't my first and likely not my last."

"Civilian life is lot looser," you offer. "And who wouldn't pay good gold for a pilot and warmage for mercenary work?"

He looks at you hard. "I've got a soft spot for airmen."

"Sounds like life will be all desk jobs then." You wink.

YOU MAY STOP HERE AND GO TO BED. IF SO, YOU HEAL 20 VITALITY AND GO TO THE NEXT SCENE.

OTHERWISE, FOR ROMANCE, CONTINUE BELOW.

You two kiss for a few minutes.

Your shirts comes off. He's a model of military service. Mercifully, he's also quiet.

He pushes you down on the bed.

You look up to him as he pulls out his belt but he leaves his trousers on.

You start to speak, but he puts his finger to his lips, suggesting you stay quiet.

He folds the belt to make a restraint.

After a few minutes of amusing play like this, you two collapse on the bed together and enjoy a genuine kiss.

He's pleasant. Clearly, however, he's also drunk and will deliver no actual fun tonight. All too soon, he passes out. You figure it's probably for the best and hope you two forget most of this by morning.

YOU SLEEP DEEPLY AND HEAL 30 VITALITY POINTS!

GO TO THE NEXT SCENE.

PART VIII

A MONSTER
IN MOST TIME ZONES

Scene #33

Thank You & Goodbye

It's morning, 0800 hours. You've rested. You push out of your mind that you might really be some kind of superhero. Whatever the truth, you have someone special to save now.

In your quarters' loo at the mirror, you grasp the jade cross that the parson gave you. As you focus, you suffer no nausea and no whispers or urges tug at you.

In the mirror, you rewind your life back to Command School and visualize yourself learning the *Erase* spell rather than... *Hmm, what must I forget in its place? Light, Charm,* or *Aim?* No, you pick a minor protection spell you rarely use.

As knowledge of the *Erase* spell crystallizes in your mind, a scar appears on your right hand. It is from a school fencing duel that memory now reports you lost rather than won.

You head to the infirmary, gathering Mancy and Slacks as you go, and Doc Rabbit leads you to the incoherent mage. You whisper in his ear, "We'll get you right as rain, Papa."

"*Deleo!*" you cry to erase the sigil etched onto his chest.

TRY AN ACT OF AGILITY.
(X=D20 + 3 IF AGILITY IS A GIFT.

———————————————

YOU FAIL IF X IS LESS THAN 9:

The spell fizzles. You refocus and try again. "*Deleo!*"

YOU EXPEND 1 VITALITY. YOU MUST KEEP TRYING AND EXPENDING VITALITY UNTIL YOU SUCCEED.

———————————————

WHEN YOU SUCCEED:

The sigil vanishes. Mage Greene sputters a bit as he returns to lucidity. As if in the middle of a thought, he speaks, "... and I've been dabbling in dark spirits, you see..."

"Yes, Doomed Salu'im," you say, excited he is alert.

"Why yes." He is surprised you know. He looks around confused as if unaware that he had gone mad.

"I did a few minutes of investigating," you explain. "And brought you back. Well, Mancy found you." You smile at her.

"No doubt, Special Lieutenant," he replies and smiles too. "So sorry for the need to restrain me and all," he offers.

Slacks interjects, "Let him finish the story."

"Ah yes," Mage Greene continues. "I thought the spirit could greatly boost Mad Muse, and it did, but that bugger of a spirit has a mind of its own and is a wee bit sharper than me."

"What happened?" you ask.

"I channeled the spirit into the whole ship. The Redkite jumped ahead several minutes in time to Paladin's Point."

"The spirit jumps through time?" you ask, amazed.

"Yes, but then the ergo went crazy and everyone ended up... well, I can't say where we winked out to. The ship flew on, leaving us behind, free-falling."

"And you all smashed into rocks below," Mancy adds.

"Did any of our Redkite's men survive?" he asks.

Your wan smile and shaking head deliver the bad news. Tears well up in your eyes and his.

"I over-reached," he laments. "If you learn anything, remember the danger of dabbling with dark magic." You start to get angry that he blames himself. He is your teacher, your father these years and your hero.

"True but listen," you want to explain. "That Nyquist guy with the box—it wasn't your fault, you couldn't have known—that box, uh, amplifies the gradient of magical potential, or something like that...."

Mage Greene smiles. "That is the nature of these little boo-boos. We can't have known."

"Perhaps," you reply. "I couldn't have reached this point

without every lesson you taught me." You hold back your tears.

He stares at you, unblinking. Your eyes lock. His tongue is held mute, as if his mind is briefly frozen in time.

"Listen, we're almost at my train stop," he says pointedly.

"I will fix this," you insist. "I'll fix this, Papa."

He smiles warmly at you. "Anything else?" he asks.

"I'm a..." you start. You want to tell him that you might be some kind of comic book hero, but you don't want to utter something so crazy sounding in front of Slacks and Mancy.

"Keep up, kid," Mage Greene exhorts. He often said that phrase when you were younger, so you would focus on courage.

You find some words. "Mr. Nyquist is saying some really crazy stuff about my magical potential."

"You do love comic books," he says. He briefly twists in pain as if currents of lightning or eels are running through him. "Seems wildly unlikely. But what did I teach you? Statistically, nothing is impossible." He turns to Slacks and Mancy. "Watch over this young one, will you."

They are taking it all in.

"One little detail," he adds, "I see you've erased that sigil on me. It bound the spirit. It acts as a 'seal' because, you know, it seals something in. Just a little warning for what..." He spasms again and his mouth foams green ooze.

"Doc! Do something!" you beg.

Doc Rabbit raises his hands, "This is beyond me."

"Wait, wait!" You plead to the mage. "Stay with us!"

Mancy comes over and asks him, "The flight, the spirit, a time jump, it was all pre-authorized, wasn't it?"

"Smart cookie," he replies to her and winks. His eyes gleam. They glaze over. His breathing gets shallow, almost inaudible. To you, he whispers, "Love you, my child."

He breathes his last and expires.

Before you can shed tears, his chest heaves up as if something is churning inside of him, ready to get out.

GO TO THE NEXT SCENE.

SCENE #34

CORPSE FLOWER

The lights flicker. The face of Mage Greene's corpse is frozen in knowing the horror of his end. Something squirms within him.

The Doc applies his stethoscope.

"Anything?" you ask.

"A heartbeat," he says, "but irregular, not a goliath's or human's heart, and maybe two hearts…"

Slacks says, "He was more shell than man in the end."

The Doc agrees. "I suspect we were talking to an impression or a loop of his final thoughts rather than his actual…"

"Hey," Mancy says, noticing a detail. "You hear that?"

A quiet, gentle mechanical hum echoes through the room. The rabbits in the Doc's hutch get skittish and retreat to the back of their little home as the hum grows louder.

"That's not from any of my equipment," Doc says.

"Look," Mancy says, pointing to a tray of metal surgical tools. They vibrate. They slowly slide—dance—in the direction of the mage's corpse. One falls and clatters on the tile floor.

Mage Greene's torso heaves up from his sacrum to the base of his neck as if possessed. Green goo erupts from his mouth. "Vooosh," he babbles.

"What the frick…" Slacks says, pulling out his pistol.

The guard at the door aims his rifle. "That ain't right!" he exclaims. "He unlocks his rifle and holds it steady, aiming at the gymnastic corpse.

"*Protegus me*," Slacks incants to cloak himself with a magical shield. You would normally cast that spell too but you chose to retroactively unlearn it to know *Erase* instead.

The lights die and the room goes dark.

You hear vibrating, a clanking… gasping breathing, then heavy breathing. Mage Greene is breathing? Or something is…

"*Fiat lux!*" you whisper, conjuring magical light above.

Mage Greene's corpse floats above the table. Wisps of black smoke and greenish tendrils push out slowly from his corpse. They explore the air and nudge the equipment around them, as if testing the space, as they stretch out ever-longer. You swear you can see starlight in the smoke.

You rub your charm and whisper "*Fateor*". The corpse and the space around it alight to your eyes with a magical aura. The aura is the shape of a womb. The aura should reveal the general kind of magic and give a clue.

"He's turning into something?" Slacks asks you.

You shake your head no. "It's a gateway," you reply.

The corpse slams down on the exam table and the tendrils go limp. They shrivel up and turn to smoke.

The lights wink back to normal.

You slowly and deeply utter a sigh of sigh relief. You were holding your breath the whole time. The others follow suit.

The Doc rushes over to power up his x-ray machine while Mancy pulls her zap rifle off her back and preps it.

"You firing that in here?" Slacks asks disapprovingly.

"Not yet," she replies, eager yet sensible.

"The x-ray machine's batteries are dead too," Doc adds.

BWOOM! An explosion hits you.

You're hot and damp. Black smoke obscures the room.

The guard fires at the exam table where the corpse should be. A tendril flies around and slices his head clean off.

"Agh!!!" the Doc screams. "Get it off m…" He's somewhere in the smoke. You hear a choking sound.

SILENCE.

Slacks starts to mouth something, but Mancy puts her finger to her lips to shush him.

As the black smoke clears, you make out the floor. The tiles barely peak through shiny black blood and piles of gory skin-stuff like the remains of some monstrous amniotic sack.

Only your magical light provides illumination.

A klaxon blares in the distance. You know that with the

klaxon, steel doors will have closed off this section. You can't seem to speak. Or you can't hear yourself speak. Maybe you lost your hearing in the explosion?

You take tentative steps closer to the exam table, your shotgun Red Silver in hand. You spot movement. A child-sized biped—an amalgam of traits—squats on the floor over the Doc's body. It's ripping apart the poor man. It's testing and chewing on pieces of his flesh. It spits out a big piece. "*Glaaah!*" it cries.

TRY AN ACT OF AGILITY.
(X=D20 + 3 IF AGILITY IS A GIFT.)

YOU FAIL IF X IS LESS THAN 15:

You slip on the gory slick floor and land on your butt. Your shotgun bounces out of your hands as you catch yourself. It lands a good five feet away. The gore burns like acid.

The little monster toddles over to you. "*Hluk hluk!*" It sniffs its way. Its tentacles quiver eagerly but it holds back. It has big black orbs for eyes and a devil's horns. You look away.

You roll to get away, grab your gun, and get up.

YOU LOSE 1D6 VITALITY POINTS AND 1 SANITY POINT.
YOU MUST RETRY THIS SECTION UNTIL YOU SUCCEED.

WHEN YOU SUCCEED:

Mancy makes hand signs for tactical instructions.

You and Slacks retreat. You cover the storage door while Slacks covers the exit to the corridor.

FLAM! The creature smashes past Slacks and out into the corridor.

GO TO THE NEXT SCENE.

Scene #35

Terrible Choice

You three chase the creature into the corridor. The klaxon is louder now, an unhappy sign of your improved hearing.

Lights are flickering wildly.

At a ceiling outlet some twenty away, the creature suckles from a smashed lamp like a Hell-spawned piglet at a sow's tit.

"What the...?" Slacks starts.

The body of a nurse and middle-aged vet in a toppled wheelchair lay crumpled and bloody on the floor.

You rush over, "Get me a potion or med kit," you yell. They are still and gray with small holes that ooze.

The creature stops its suckling, stares at you, and flees—or just moves on?—hopping back and forth along the ceiling down the corridor in a chaotic path. Its motion is jittery, like blips and skips on a record player or film reel.

Slacks stops, stretches out his arm, points at the creature, and incants, *"Radius ignis ardescit."* A pencil-thin ruby ray makes its way to the creature and blossoms into a ball of fire.

As the blistering flames clear, the creature looks unscathed. It angrily hisses in your direction and continues.

"Where's it going?" Slacks asks as you three run.

"My odds are on the power plant," Mancy replies.

"Don't let it get outside!" you urge.

You three follow it around a bend.

A guard and two technicians are holding their ground—or cowering upright—in front of a pair of steel doors. A thick glass pane in the door reveals the huge power plant room beyond. The guard is firing his rifle at the creature but missing or maybe hitting to no effect.

"Airmen!" Mancy cries to get their attention as she hoists her zap rifle, "duck!"

Slacks touches it and incants, "*Maximize potestate!*"

You try to add your own touch but something pulls you back as the creature's tentacles slash into the three defenders. They crumple, instantly slain, just as Mancy fires. *Zzzzzzit!*

From her gun, a storm of electricity blasts a 15-ft spread and wallops the creature, flinging it to the floor. It tumbles back onto its butt and tries to stagger up, confused and enraged.

A moaning ash-colored nurse grapples you to the floor. Her grip is incredibly strong. The slain vet and decapitated guard from the infirmary both eagerly shamble toward you.

TRY AN ACT OF BRAWN.
(X=D20 + 3 IF BRAWN IS A GIFT.

YOU FAIL IF X IS LESS THAN 9:

You struggle to break free of the zombie nurse as she grapples and claws at you and spits acidic goo.

YOU LOSE 1D6 VITALITY POINTS AND 1 SANITY POINT. YOU MUST RETRY THIS SECTION UNTIL YOU SUCCEED.

WHEN YOU SUCCEED:

You blast the zombie nurse with your shotgun square in the head and break free.

Mancy fires her zap rifle again at the creature. *Zzzzzzit!*

The creature lashes out with its razor tentacles at Mancy and Slacks. They will surely die unless you act. Who do you shove out of the way to safety?

IF YOU SAVE MANCY, GO TO SCENE #36A
(PAGE 130). OR, IF YOU SAVE SLACKS,
GO TO SCENE #36B (PAGE 132).

SCENE #36A

YOU AND MANCY

The creature has vanished. The power plant doors are shut tight. Zombies are closing in. It's now up to you and Mancy.

She wastes no time turning her zap rifle on the zombies. She yells, "Die plonkers!" as she blows them away repeatedly until the rifle malfunctions. All that's left are charred ex-undead.

She angrily tosses her rifle to the side. "Crykke!"

Slacks is slumped over on the ground. You try to resuscitate him but he has multiple tentacle punctures to his chest, neck, and head. He's gone, and likely another zombie soon.

The klaxons continue to wail.

Mancy turns to you, takes in Slacks's corpse, and asks, "Where did that bastard go?"

She scans the corridor for broken ventilation ducts, bloody tracks, and the like. The left end of the corridor is sealed by emergency doors, while the right end leads to an underground command center. All is still and quiet there. She peers through the door glass into the power plant. The technicians there look terrified but also relieved. They shrug at her shouts to them.

"Where did it go?" she asks you.

You shake your head. But you consider...in your mind's eye, you zoom through all the details of the creature that you can remember. Yes, you're sure its skin was etched with a sigil of Doomed Salu'im. Thus, it should have that spirit's power.

"The question is not where, but when," you tell her.

She stares at you a long while.

"Who did this?" she asks. "Who fricked us?"

You wonder how much you can or should say. Your mind is hardly working anyway. The carnage overwhelms you.

"Mage Greene made a mistake," you finally reply.

"Bullocks," she replies. "It was that slimy Calv, isn't it?"

One thing you've learned in your short time knowing Mancy is that others' hidden motives rarely escape her keen senses.

"Sort of. Calv didn't help, that's true," you offer.

She breathes out hard, repeatedly, and calms herself. "Frick," she curses as exhaustion catches up to her.

"Listen Mancy," you say seriously, "I estimate we've got a few minutes at most, maybe..." If it's the spirit of Doomed Salu'im, it will bounce through time like the Redkite did.

The power plant doors open. The technicians emerge, excessively eager to exit the building.

"Lieutenant, we all clear?" a skinny one with glasses asks.

"No!" you warn them. Your own anger and tugs of hysteria are finally boiling up. "Quickly, get back and close the..."

The creature reappears, as if just popping in.

It moves at full speed like a bird passing by a window or like a stone skipping across a pond. It scrambles into the power plant room and vanishes, again.

"Agh!" the technician exclaims. "No way we're going back in there!"

Slacks' corpse grabs you. He growls. You bash at him.

TRY AN ACT OF BRAWN.
(X=D20 + 3 IF BRAWN IS A GIFT.

YOU FAIL IF X IS LESS THAN 9:

You shake and push off zombie Slacks, then wince as you put him down with a shotgun blast to his head.

YOU LOSE 1D6 VITALITY POINTS AND 1 SANITY POINT. YOU MUST RETRY THIS SECTION UNTIL YOU SUCCEED.

WHEN YOU SUCCEED:

"Sorry C," Mancy says kindly as you push off the corpse.

"It's not over." You worry the creature will return.

You consider, *What would Mage Greene do?* Well, maybe he wouldn't know the right answer. After all, he was the one messing with dark magic in the first place. *Whatever.* You will cast the best spell or do whatever it takes to make everyone safe.

"I'm going into the power plant chamber," you tell Mancy, "and I want you to close the doors behind me."

"You sure?"

"Yes." You have scant idea if you can actually take down this creature but you have a plan that's simple but workable.

You walk in.

GO TO SCENE #37 (PAGE 135).

SCENE #36B

YOU AND SLACKS

The creature has vanished. The power plant doors are shut tight. Zombies are closing in. It's now up to you and Slacks.

Slacks wastes no time. He grabs you, pulls you with him as he steps back, and incants, "*Radius ignis ardescit!*" As before, a pencil-thin ruby ray makes its way to the zombies and blossoms into a ball of fire. All that's left are charred ex-undead.

"Bloody Nine Hells!" he shouts. "You okay, C?" he asks.

"Yeah." You're dazed.

Mancy is on the ground. You kneel and try to resuscitate her but she's got multiple tentacle punctures to her chest, neck, and head. She's gone and likely she'll be another zombie soon.

The klaxons continue to wail.

Slacks briefly looks around, sees nothing more, and asks, "Where did that bloody monster go?"

You consider... In your mind's eye, you zoom through all the details of the creature you can remember. Yes, you're sure its skin was etched with a sigil of Doomed Salu'im. Thus, it should have that spirit's power.

"The question is not where, but when," you tell him.

"What?"

"I'm not totally certain," you explain, "but I think it skipped ahead in time, maybe up to five minutes."

"That's crazy talk, C," he replies, unbelieving. "You've got a concussion." He holds up his hand with some fingers up. "How many fingers am I holding up?"

"Um, three fingers," you reply confidently.

"Listen, you remember the Redkite." You walk Slacks through the evidence. "You were there when Mage Greene said the spirit moved the whole ship ahead five minutes in time. Like poof, and then it reappeared."

"Half of Greene's brain was goo," Slacks says, "and we don't really know what happened to the log. It was a mess."

You consider maybe Slacks has a good point. Maybe the creature is just... You wrack your brain to recall something useful from your magic theory class at Command School.

"It'll bet you five premium coffees it's just invisible," Slacks offers.

"And doing what?" you ask incredulously.

"How should I know," he says. "Maybe it's looking for a way out." He sounds like he's trying to convince himself.

You recall what Mage Greene babbled just yesterday, and tell Slacks, "It skips like a stone across a pond."

The power plant doors open. The technicians emerge, excessively eager to exit the building.

"Lieutenant, we all clear?" a skinny one in glasses asks.

"No!" you warn them. Your own anger and tugs of hysteria are finally boiling up. "Quickly, get back and close the..."

The creature reappears, as if just popping in.

It moves at full speed like a bird passing by a window or

like a stone skipping across a pond. It scrambles into the power plant room and vanishes, again.

"Agh?!" the technician exclaims. "Not going back, Sir!"

Mancy's corpse grabs you. You bash at her.

TRY AN ACT OF BRAWN.
(X=D20 + 3 IF BRAWN IS A GIFT.

YOU FAIL IF X IS LESS THAN 9:

You shake and push off zombie Mancy, then wince as you put her down with a shotgun blast to the head.

YOU LOSE 1D6 VITALITY AND 1 SANITY. YOU MUST RETRY THIS SECTION UNTIL YOU SUCCEED.

WHEN YOU SUCCEED:

"Sorry C," Slacks says kindly as you push off the corpse.

"It's not over." You worry the creature will return.

"Then let's have it!" Slacks exclaims.

You consider, *What would Mage Greene do?* Well, maybe he wouldn't know the right answer. After all, he was the one messing with dark magic in the first place. *Whatever.* You will cast the best spell or do whatever it takes to make everyone safe.

"I'm going into the power plant chamber," you tell Slacks, "and I want you to close the doors behind me."

"You sure?"

"Yes." You have scant idea if you can actually take down this creature, but you have a plan that's simple but workable.

You walk in.

GO TO THE NEXT SCENE.

Scene #37

Time Shift

You pace alone in the power plant chamber waiting for the creature to reappear. Your plan: When it appears, you will grab onto it and disable or kill it, ideally by magically erasing its sigil then stabbing or shooting it. Of course, as you learned in Command School, no plan survives first contact with the enemy.

The power plant is large, hot and cramped with cables, fuel lines, and furnaces. Metal catwalks crisscross a second level. You already cleared everyone out, and for a brief time, it can operate on its own. You figure, the fewer variables, the fewer victims. It's what Mage Greene would have done. It's what Mancy and Slacks would do, and the Commander too.

HOW DO YOU PREPARE? DO YOU FOCUS ON 1), GRAPPLING THE CREATURE? 2), USING MAGIC TO SUBDUE IT, 3) CHECKING YOUR GEAR, OR 4) PRAYING FOR GRIT AND GUIDANCE?

Ideally, you should have tracked the creature's arrivals and departures so far to estimate the next one, but you thought of this too late. At least you remember the creature's vector of entry and where it vanished and thus where it will surely return. You stand at that point. You check that your dagger and shotgun are easily accessible, and you prepare to cast the *Erase* spell.

Outside the doors, the survivors peer through the small glass window, sating their curiosity. You give them a thumbs up.

You wonder, what is it like for a fish to suddenly get hit, baited, or pounced from a danger above the waterline? A fish cannot see what arrives from above, can it? Smart fish sensibly stay clear of the surface, yes? Yet surely some venture to the surface, survive, and maybe even fight back. Don't they?

The creature reappears.

You grab it! To the outside observers, you vanish with it. Now you too are but an echo in the stream of time.

What's next is hard to describe. Time passes for you before you reappear, but wherever you are, it's a weird, dizzying, and chilly darkness—a soul-sucking void.

TRY AN ACT OF ENDURANCE.
(X=D20 + 3 IF ENDURANCE IS A GIFT.
ADD +2 IF YOU PREPARED BY PRAYING
FOR GRIT AND GUIDANCE.)

YOU FAIL IF X IS LESS THAN 9:

Oh Lord God Creator in Heaven!

A cacophony of lights and sounds, vistas and voices, blast at you like a galaxy of novas lighting off or a multitude of bards lamenting their lives all at once. Even as you try to focus on one vista or tune into one voice, vertigo overwhelms you, as if each is the sharp precipice of an impossible geometric space.

You cling to the creature. It smells of suffocating acrid smoke. You fear if you let go, you will surely be flung out headlong into a void of nothingness to die, or worse.

The jade amulet around your neck glows brightly as it clears the creature's smoke from your eyes and nostrils.

"Where are we?" you ask, not sure what else to say.

Its black eyes lock onto yours.

"Heir of Demos Kalagos," it calls you. Its voice is in your head. Its voice is female. "I am heir to Doomed Salu'im," it whispers, "and we are in...." She struggles for a label.

She grows large. She literally grows in size and now embraces you like a mother holds her babe against her bosom. The flagella on her chin grow into small tentacles. Her arms bulge and claws sharpen.

"What are we?"

Her tears sting your face. The beat of her heart is the ache of love betrayed. The jade amulet around your neck flashes with a star-burst as it cracks open.

"So hungry," she pines.

Off in the distance, a window of light is coming up... Is that the real world awaiting your return?

You flash through your own stories, your multiple time-lines. What if you stayed in the attic as a kid? Or didn't go to Command School? What if this creature had gone in a different direction, heading outside?

TO LEARN THE ANSWER, TURN THE PAGE TO SCENE #38, AND IF YOU SURVIVE THAT SCENE, RETURN TO THIS SCENE AND CONTINUE TO SUCCESS BELOW. OR, PURSUE NO ANSWER AND KEEP READING.

You struggle to shutter your eyes, ears, nostrils, and mind against the dizzying onslaught of alternative paths.

YOU LOSE 1 VITALITY POINT AND 1D6 SANITY POINTS. YOU MUST TRY AGAIN AND REPEAT THIS SECTION UNTIL YOU SUCCEED.

WHEN YOU SUCCEED:

You hang on with your full might as you and the creature return to the land of the living in the power plant. Like a stone at the end of its journey, you two smash back into reality.

"Thanks for joining," it whispers. "You get off here."

"*Deleo*", you incant, erasing the sigil on it.

It looks at you, betraying nothing you understand.

"This is for Greene," you pronounce. Your shotgun, Red Silver, has the final say right at the creature's forehead.

GO TO SCENE #39 (PAGE 139).

Scene #38

Out in the Moors

In this alternate timeline, you, Mancy, and Slacks have been out roaming the moors. Above you, clouds are heavy with imminent rain. Lightning thrashes.

The three of you now face off with the horrid creature. Back at base, it smashed through a ventilation shaft to get free. You tracked it to the shell of a half-drowned plane, and from there it emerged after a blast of lightning struck the fuselage. By whatever magic or unnatural metabolism, it has now grown huge and terrible, some 20 feet high, out-matching you all. It grabs at you.

Try an Act of Brawn.
(X=D20 + 3 if Brawn is a gift.)

You fail if X is less than 15:

There is no where to hide as it grabs, crushes, and tries to swallow each of you in turn.

You lose 3D6 vitality and 1D6 sanity points.
Repeat this section until you succeed.
If you die in this section,
you cannot recover by any means.

When you succeed:

You regain your equilibrium. You remember this is all just a potential possibility of what might have been!

If you live, return to the previous scene.

Scene #39

Examination

You kneel down to closely inspect the monster's sprawling corpse, aiming to learn as much as you can. Even as you do so, like dry ice, it is starting to dissipate, its bloated body sublimating into a dank, shadowy gas.

It is humanoid but far from human or any other mortal ancestry. Its stitched from a motley mix of parts: a pair of devil's horns, aberrant webbed feet and hands off of gangly legs and arms, bat-like wings sprouting from its hunched back, a savage skull-like head with large, brutal opal eyes, jagged white teeth, an uncouth snout, and a "beard" of tentacles that still writhe like flagella in their own death throes.

Despite chills and revulsion, you exert sheer will to use a knife and kerchief to analyze it, pushing past its acidic blood.

Try an Act of Intellect.
(X=D20 + 3 if Intellect is a gift.)

You fail if X is less than 9:

You get lost in its empty eyes, drowning into cold, dizzying nothingness. Your mind reels as you spiral into nightmares. You shiver and sweat as you wander confused in darkness. At times, there are masses of others like you, barking and screaming as if struggling under the weight of a great boot of eternity. Desperately, you hang on to a sliver of sanity, the photograph of Mage Greene and his lost family, as you search for a way out of a dark, pulsing, blistering void.

Yes, there! You spy a pinpoint of light like a window in a dark mansion. Like a rat, you find your way to the light, open the window, and scamper out.

YOU LOSE 1D6 SANITY POINTS AND 1 VITALITY POINT AS YOU CONTINUE TO BLEED.

YOU MUST TRY AGAIN UNTIL YOU SUCCEED. IF YOU FAIL AGAIN, REPEAT THIS SECTION.

WHEN YOU SUCCEED:

You steel your mind to focus, suppressing your natural mortal reactions to dispassionately examine it.

Looking closely, you see signs of intelligence and social organization. It wears rags. Thusly, it is aware of itself and suffers shame. It sports piercings, scars, tattoos, and other body modifications. There are kills as skulls, a heart as love, and stars as…? These suggest fear, love, guilt, and other sentiments.

"What are you?" you ask its still form.

Standing back, and mentally subtracting out its tentacle "beard", you discern a mockery of Mage Greene's face.

"Or who are you?"

Some kind of metal tool sticks halfway out of its rough, stinking torso. Carefully you draw forth the tool. It is a giant multi-purpose device akin to a scout's. It holds a knife, spoon, pliers, and screwdriver. You wonder what it eats. And surely there are more like it, perhaps a whole horrific civilization.

With concerted prodding, you realize the tool is one of several stored in a fleshy drawer akin to a marsupial's pouch.

And there it is: A near-invisible imprint wraps around its body. It is a geometric seal, the sigil of Doomed Salu'im.

You fumble in your pockets for a vial or similar container to hold a sample but find nothing. All too quickly, its flesh and tools vanish as if it had never existed.

THAT NIGHT, YOU SLEEP POORLY, HEALING ONLY 5 VITALITY POINTS. GO TO THE NEXT SCENE.

PART IX

YOU'VE ARRIVED
AT YOUR DESTINATION

Scene #40

Mage Greene's Funeral

A few days later, that Friday at noon, you deliver the blessing at Mage Greene's funeral. While some knew him well, you knew him best. Perhaps not fitting the mood, the sun is out and the day is warm.

You read through your prepared speech. It's all a blur as memories and tears overtake you.

Next, you must give the holy blessing. Normally, the parson does this. But you feel a calling a do the blessing yourself.

Try an Act of Faith.
(X=D20 + 3 if Faith is a gift.)

You fail if X is less than 9:

You wiff the blessing and must try harder to get it right.

You expend 1 vitality to recast the blessing. Repeat this section until you succeed.

When you succeed:

The blessing feels like a success. After a moment, everyone nods in approval. Mostly, you feel deeply relieved. The blessing is not simply to assist the dead in their afterlife. That is the Almighty's responsibility. The blessing lightens the weight of loss for the living, granting the light of hope for the future.

Go to the next scene.

SCENE #41

PROMOTION

You sit alone in the Commander's office. You await his arrival to officially review the events of the past week and consider what's next. The past few years come to mind even as you contemplate your future. Hopefully, you are in for a promotion and can finagle some extra perks.

The chessboard on the Commander's desk is frozen in the middle of a game. Half of its pieces are taken. You wonder who he is playing against.

From what you know of chess, the black king is now in a precarious position. But a black bishop, knight, and rook also remain. You notice a strategic sacrifice could shift the tide. This makes you think. Growing up on an airbase has impressed upon you the practical fact that in the military, people—like stories—are deployed for usefulness, and are, paradoxically, both precious and expendable. You wonder, what kind of piece are you? You are not a pawn, nor are you His Majesty King George V. Perhaps you are now a knight?

The board inspires you to brainstorm your options now. What change might give you higher pay? What would give you the chance to meet interesting people and visit new places? Or maybe you don't want any more commitments? You could use a comfortable holiday. What if...

The Commander enters. You stand at attention. He sits, waves you to join him and offers a mild smile as he activates an audio recorder as required for debriefing so that higher-ups can review if needed.

HOW DO YOU APPROACH THIS MEETING? DO YOU FOCUS ON BEING 1) AMBITIOUS, 2) EXCITED, 3) HUMBLE, 4) QUESTIONING, OR 5) TIRED?

```
        Royal Air Force
  Letter of Special Investigation
```

16 March 1936

Dear Comdr. Hollingsworth,

The attached dossier regards the mysterious loss of all persons aboard spellship Redkite after it departed our base three days prior. The investigation is concluded. Herein is a summary of the key discoveries and resolution.

Redkite departed that morning as scheduled with a spellpilot, twelve airmen, and Major Mage Greene. Redkite radioed in earlier than expected at a key way-point and returned soon after with no crew. All cargo was present including an ergo, a technocrat (aka 'Mad Muse'), and a strongbox with unknown but cleared civilian contents.

Mage Greene cast a spell to improve the technocrat. This spell conjured a spirit. He lost control of the spirit, and it took control of the spellship. By unknown means, it dumped the airmen and Mage Greene into empty air. Except for the mage, they all fell to their deaths near Paladin's Peak. Lt. Mancy and her team found and retrieved them all.

Mage Greene later died due to wounds inflicted by the spirit despite our best mundane and magical efforts. Upon expiring, the spirit--or its off-spring--emerged from the mage's body as a monster of unknown kind, but possibly an occult creature called a vivilor. Much effort was expended to track and defeat this monster, which "fed" upon the power in electrical cables and quickly grew to a large size. There were seven more casualities. The corpse of the monster quickly turned to dust.

There have been no further strange or deadly occurrences. The case is now closed.

Sp.Lt. C. Ernest

C. Ernest

"Ernest, you need a kick in the pants," he says as he pulls out a folder.

"Excuse me, Sir?" you reply, surprised.

"You heard me. I'm proud of you. You've done a bang-up job. And now it's time to boot you out of this small corner of the Commonweal to what suits your skills and our King's needs."

"That's quite forthright of you, Sir."

"Mmm." He pages through the folder. It includes the recent case, including your sanitized reports. You couldn't mention Royal Cabinet. "Looks less grim from afar, and you solved the mystery and slew the monster." He looks up expectantly.

"Um..." You're not sure what he expects. "I've grown up here and it's my home, my family, and I was defending all of us."

"We've enjoyed hosting you." The Commander smiles warmly. He closes the folder. "I've put in a request to promote you to Field Investigator and reassign you to Royal Cabinet. You can travel all over the world.

"Thank you, Sir." You expected a promotion, but not reassignment.

"You handled yourself well. We don't want you to leave. You're an asset and comfortable here. But I see your potential."

Your stomach flips with excitement. This is a chance to experience different cultures and races, ancient and famous places, and meet and learn from other amazing investigators like Dr. Joan Carver. And you figure, whether by post or telephone, he can stay in touch with your mates here. In the past, the prospect of world travel intimidated you. But you survived Command School, a time-shifting monster, and Calv's secret box. Whether or not you're actually a super hero, now is a time for adventure, and to maybe reach for more.

"Yes, Field Investigator?" the Commander asks.

TRY AN ACT OF CHARM.
(X=D20 + 3 IF CHARM IS A GIFT.
ADD +5 IF YOU FOCUS ON STAYING HUMBLE.)

YOU FAIL IF X IS LESS THAN 9:

"May I make a suggestion?" the Commander says, thumbing off the recorder.

"Of course," you reply.

"Now is the time to ask me for a perk."

"What do you mean?"

"To sweeten the deal, if you know what I mean, when I restart the recorder."

"Gosh, I don't know. That's very generous of you."

"Maybe give it a minute," the Commander says. "You rarely ask for anything for yourself. Now is a chance to practice. You'll need it." He moves to thumb on the recorder.

YOU EXPEND 1 VITALITY TO PUT IN MORE EFFORT. REPEAT THIS SECTION UNTIL YOU SUCCEED.

WHEN YOU SUCCEED:

"You know, Commander, I am special," you pipe up with confidence. "Perhaps I could get a flight pass to give out once a year to a friend or colleague..."

The Commander nods approvingly.

"... to visit me anywhere in the world. Once a year."

"A thoughtful choice," he replies.

"Nothing fancy of course. Just a flight pass."

"Of course, we're no cruise company for the hoity-toity," the Commander replies.

You both laugh at the thought. You visualize drop-kicking a Richy Rich out of a spellship, with a parachute of course.

He stands, and you follow suit and salute.

"Congratulations," he says proudly, shaking your hand.

GO TO THE NEXT SCENE.

Scene #42
In the Pilot's Seat

The heart of the Commonweal, Londinium and royal Ellencourt, comes into view over the horizon. You and Calv are in a two-seater prop plane some 3,000 ft up. You are at the helm as the pilot and he is acting as navigator. Flying him to the capitol is your first assignment as a Field Investigator.

The winds are mostly calm out of the southwest, and the sky patchy with clouds. Modest gusts rock the small plane now and then, testing your deftness. As you slowly descend to Rosewode Aeroport, a blast of wind rocks the plane violently.

Try an Act of Agility.
(X=D20 + 3 if Agility is a gift.)

You fail if X is less than 9:

You keep your cool as you channel energy into the helm and do you best to adjust this little flying contraption.

You expend 1 vitality to stabilize the plane. Repeat this section until you succeed.

When you succeed:

"Glad lunch is ahead of us," Calv jokes, slightly green.

"I'll be easier on you next time," you reply slyly. "So what's our first mission? You've kept me in the dark."

"We're going to snag a vampire or ten. Madam Mikka thinks she's escaped but I wager she'll lead us to a lovely nest."

The End.

About the Author

Dario Nardi, PhD is an author, speaker and expert in the fields of neuroscience and personality. He is also a fantasy game designer. Dario holds a senior lecturer position at the University of California (Los Angeles) where he won UCLA's Distinguished Teacher of the year in 2011. His books include *Neuroscience of Personality*, *8 Keys to Self-Leadership*, and *Jung on Yoga*, among other titles. Since 2007, Dario has conducted hands-on brain research while writing game books, starting with *Secrets of Pact Magic* and *Villains of Pact Magic,* and later co-authoring with Alexander Augunas on the full-color *Grimoire of Lost Souls*. Work on RADIANCE RPG began in 2008 and culminated in the *Radiance Players Guide* in 2012. Dario has been a fan of roleplaying games since 1982 and is excited to promote a story-driven novella that affords some of the options and rewards of tabletop RPGs. Learn more at www.DarioNardi.com.

BEHIND THE SCENES

You can go through *Echoes in the Stream of Time* as a stand-alone gamebook. However, it is also a puzzle piece in a larger series with an as-yet opaque story arc, and the puzzle includes a psychological dimension. Here is a glimpse behind the scenes as a reward for your work.

The world of O'arth is similar to our own 1930s but with the twist of actual magic spells and literal monsters. Among these is the option to summon and bind powerful spirits of yore. In this series' first book, *Night Journey of the Soul,* the hero d'Luminar binds multiple spirits for brief periods. For him, changing spirits is like changing hats. In contrast, here, Ernest is permanently bound with one spirit, Demos Kalagos. This makes our hero an *heirian*—an heir to a spirit's power and this world's version of a comic book superhero. Exactly how or why this happens to Ernest (and a few others) is for future discovery.

If you compare this book to *Night Journey of the Soul,* you will find many other similarities and differences. For example, the adventures occur close in time but in different places. Both grant a glimpse of a major villain, the pactmaker vampire Mikka, and highlight the good and bad intentions and consequences of pactmaking.

Beyond a surface comparison, investigator d'Luminar and airman Ernest have different personalities and the reading experience reflects that. In *Night Journey of the Soul,* as the hero d'Luminar, you are a practical and adaptable realist, and while you are a loner hardened to misery, you are also principled and act for others beyond yourself. Akin to d'Luminar's personality, the scenes are short on dialog and filled with quick action, problem solving, and tactical options in the face of many dangers and familiar kinds of foes like zombies. In contrast, here in *Echoes in the Stream of Time* as Ernest, you are somewhat naive like a skiff at the mercy of a coming storm. You are also rooted in your past and relationships, benefit from others for approval and guidance, and prefer company. Reflecting Ernest's personality, the scenes are long on dialog and social maneuvering with less combat and fewer choices along a more linear path, though the choices you do make are profound.

Going deeper, both books task us to engage a hero's dark side. D'Luminar literally delves beneath a ruined church to slay literal monsters. In the process, you deal with alcohol abuse, confront a past failure, and save a child. Here, Ernest is in a familiar place and mostly deals with intangibles. In the process, you deal with a weakness for thievery, delve the basement of your memory, and take flight like a little bird leaving its nest. For each character, there is a darkness to explore and overcome.

The famous psychiatrist Dr. C.G. Jung described psychology as an alchemical process akin to magic. In life, people tend to come to rely on one-sided behaviors as they reject unwanted sides of themselves (inner demons). As they push one-sidedness, an opposing force arises and a tension develops that can simmer for years or come quickly to a boil. Imagine a pressure cooker. A way to resolve that tension before it cooks us to death is to recognize and actively engage it. Besides wholesome horrors and good fun, the stories in this series mirror that process.

FOR USE IN A TABLETOP GAME

As described in book #1, *Night Journey of the Soul*, you can use this book as the basis for your favorite tabletop role-playing game. You might use *Grimoire of Lost Souls* and *Age of Electrotech* for the PATHFINDER ROLEPLAYING GAME by Paizo Inc. Or you might use *Radiance Pact Magic* for RADIANCE RPG by Radiance House. The latter's core rule book, *Radiance Players Guide*, is available for free online (www.radiancerpg.com). RADIANCE RPG mixes magic and technology in the same historical era as this book. Regardless of which system you use, Ernest's time-bending power comes from a permanent pact with the spirit of Demos Kalagos as described on page 106.

More Books

Here are some other fiction and gaming books by this author that might interest you.

RADIANCE PLAYERS GUIDE is a stand-alone tabletop roleplaying game with streamlined mechanics and a turn-of-the-last-century atmosphere that offers electro-tech, gunslingers, magic, nations, newspapers, radio, robots, and of course monsters.

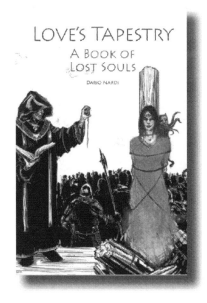

LOVE'S TAPESTRY is an anthology of over 40 tragic legends of how the spirits came to be, including Cave Mother and Angel Kaiya described here in *Night Journey of the Soul.*

GRIMOIRE OF LOST SOULS is a massive full color supplement for use with the award-winning Path-finder Roleplaying Game by Paizo Inc. It details over 120 spirits for game play plus much more.

MAP: REDKITE SPELLSHIP

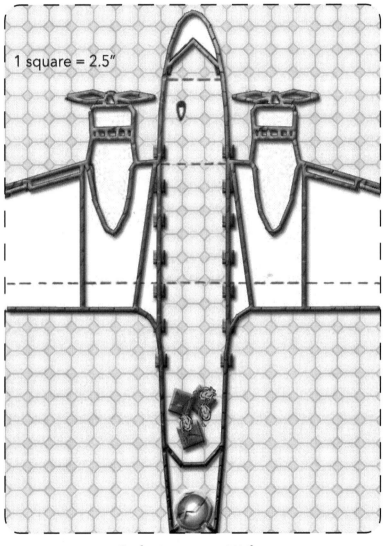

1 square = 2.5″

Scale: 1 square = 2½ feet

Note: Layout may have changed during or after fabrication,
and sections may have been repurposed since its roll-out.

Made in the USA
Las Vegas, NV
02 January 2021

15165572R00085